"What are you doing up at this hour?"

Bethany looked around to find Chandler standing in the doorway, his boots in his hand. Her heart racing, she gasped. "You frightened me."

"Sorry." He walked across the floor in his stocking feet. "You didn't answer my question. Why aren't you asleep?"

She shrugged. "Just feeling kind of weird, I guess."

Frowning, he lifted a hand to her forehead. "Maybe you're coming down with something."

"I'm fine." She reached up to remove his hand from her brow. The baby suddenly moved. Bethany instinctively placed Chandler's hand on her abdomen. "I'm not the only one who can't sleep."

He stared at her belly as it rippled, little hillocks appearing here and there, only to smooth out again as the baby moved. Finally the baby subsided into stillness, and Chandler looked up at her with awe in his cinnamon eyes.

"Amazing," Chandler whispered.

Their gazes held for several moments before he abruptly snatched his hand away.

If only, she thought, *if only this was a true marriage.*

Books by Arlene James

Love Inspired

*The Perfect Wedding
*An Old-Fashioned Love
*A Wife Worth
   Waiting For
*With Baby in Mind
To Heal a Heart
Deck the Halls
A Family to Share
Butterfly Summer
A Love So Strong
When Love Comes Home
A Mommy in Mind
**His Small-Town Girl

**Her Small-Town Hero
**Their Small-Town Love
†Anna Meets Her Match
†A Match Made in Texas
A Mother's Gift
   "Dreaming of a Family"
†Baby Makes a Match

*Everyday Miracles
**Eden, OK
†Chatam House

ARLENE JAMES

says, "Camp meetings, mission work and church attendance permeate my Oklahoma childhood memories. It was a golden time, which sustains me yet. However, only as a young widowed mother did I truly begin growing in my personal relationship with the Lord. Through adversity, He has blessed me in countless ways, one of which is a second marriage so loving and romantic it still feels like courtship!"

The author of more than seventy novels, Arlene James now resides outside Dallas, Texas, with her beloved husband. Her need to write is greater than ever, a fact that frankly amazes her, as she's been at it since the eighth grade. She loves to hear from readers, and can be reached via her Web site at www.arlenejames.com.

Baby Makes a Match
Arlene James

Steeple
Hill®

Published by Steeple Hill Books™

STEEPLE HILL BOOKS

Steeple Hill®

Recycling programs
for this product may
not exist in your area.

ISBN-13: 978-0-373-87619-8

BABY MAKES A MATCH

Copyright © 2010 by Deborah Rather

www.SteepleHill.com

Printed in U.S.A.

Then Jesus lifted up His eyes, and seeing a great multitude coming toward Him, He said to Philip, "Where shall we buy bread, that these may eat?" But this He said to test him, for He Himself knew what He would do.

—*John* 6:5–6

For Lisa Onvani,
friend, artist, beautiful soul.
Thank you,
DAR

Chapter One

"Six hundred dollars?" Bethany gaped at the mechanic. The man was unknown to her, just the first possible help that she had found along the road to Dallas after steam had started pouring out from under the hood of her pathetic little heap. "You've got to be kidding. The car wasn't worth six hundred bucks when I started out in it!"

The hulking fellow wiped grease from his hands with a grimy red cloth. "Can't argue with that," he agreed, eyeing the offending vehicle.

"Look, I'm not even going as far as Dallas," she pleaded, clutching the thin cotton skirt of her empire-style, ankle-length, blue-and-white-flowered sundress, inadvertently pulling the fabric taut across her distended belly. Her slenderness made her look further along in her pregnancy than she actually was, but she didn't think about that now. "Isn't there something you can do to get me to Buffalo Creek?"

He scratched his bald head. "Tell you what, I'll give you three hundred cash for it as is. Maybe I can part it out, get my money back that way."

"Three hundred?" Bethany repeated in dismay.

Making three hundred dollars beat shelling out six hundred that she did not even have, but how was she to make it to

Buffalo Creek if she sold her car? The baby moved, producing an odd fluttering sensation inside her abdomen, as if to say she might as well get on with it. She wasn't going anywhere in a broken-down car that she couldn't fix, anyway, so she really had no choice here. That didn't solve the problem, though. She shook her head, trying to see another way.

The tubby, middle-aged man spread his hands, displaying sweat stains on his coveralls. Bethany didn't know how he managed to work in this old garage in the stifling July heat.

"Sorry. Best I can do," he said. "You can always get a bus ticket at the diner next door."

Well, that was better than nothing, she supposed. Sighing, she shook back her dark hair and smoothed her hands over her mounded belly, feeling a cramp building.

The cramps had started a couple weeks ago, at only five months into her pregnancy. She had attributed them to stress. Lately, her life had consisted of reeling blow after reeling blow. This was just one more.

Trying to look on the bright side, she reminded herself that three hundred bucks would more than double her pathetic bankroll. Besides, it was really her only option. She could take the money and buy a bus ticket or sit beside the road until she grew roots here, just a couple hours from her brother.

"Thank you very much," she said quietly, accepting the offer. "I appreciate your help."

"I'll get your cash."

While the mechanic went for the money, Bethany opened the trunk on her old car, lifting out the smaller of her two suitcases. Thankfully, she'd had sense enough to pack up her important papers, including the title to the car, which she'd bought used way back in high school.

Eight years later, she was afoot again, but she didn't suppose she could complain about that. The car had been far more dependable and serviceable than anything or anyone else in her life. She was sorry to see it go, sorry enough to feel tears gathering.

So, what else was new? She'd cried so much lately that it would have been easier to count the minutes she *hadn't* wept.

The mechanic returned with a receipt and a stack of bills. Bethany signed over the title before going back to the car for the remainder of her belongings. He helped her wrestle the larger suitcase out of the trunk. Stacking the smaller piece of luggage atop the larger one, she pulled up the handle, unlocked the wheels and rolled the lot out into the sweltering Texas sunshine.

Squinting, she slung her handbag over one shoulder, gathered up her hair in her free hand and trudged toward the diner. Not ten months ago, she'd chopped off her dark, sleek locks at her chin, but since she'd gotten pregnant, it now brushed her shoulders again. Thankfully, with the sun hanging low in a white-hot sky, the distance was short. She silently prayed that the wait would be also.

Lord, please, I don't want to be stranded here in this dot on the map for hours on end. Can't You help me out? I mean, after everything else that's happened, can't I get a break here? I just want to get to my brother safely. And soon.

Absently, she noticed a somewhat battered, dirty white, double-cab pickup truck, towing a large horse trailer behind, on the feeder road that ran along Highway 45. The rig slowed and turned into the eatery's parking lot. The driver obviously knew what he was doing. Plodding along, Bethany watched as he expertly maneuvered the rig into the shade of the only tree within sight, drawing up mere inches from the portable sign at the edge of the lot.

A tall, slim-hipped, light-haired cowboy with broad shoulders got out and fitted a pale, high-crowned hat onto his head before moving down the side of the trailer. She couldn't see what he was doing, but it was none of her concern. She had enough concerns of her own.

Somehow, she had to get to her brother. She didn't have anywhere to go except back to Buffalo Creek and Garrett. Her brother was the only family she had and the only person on the face of the earth who would undoubtedly help her.

The cramp suddenly seized her, radiating from her navel outward, not really painful but worrisome. She gasped, then walked on, wishing that she had called Garrett to let him know that she was coming. She hadn't thought of it in her rush to get away, and she was probably the last person in the civilized world who didn't own a cell phone. There was a phone at the convenience store where she'd worked nights and a phone in the modest little house in Humble where she had lived for the past seven years. She had reasoned that she could navigate the few blocks between them without an expensive cell phone.

Bethany staggered into the relative cool of the diner, clutching her belly through the cheap sundress with one hand. Every booth in the small, narrow building was occupied and only three of seats at the counter were vacant. She maneuvered her bags to an out-of-the-way spot near the cash register and hitched up onto the stool next to them at the near end of the counter.

A waitress, with improbably red hair coiled into a frothy bun atop her head, placed a glass of iced water in front of Bethany, who seized it gratefully and drank it straight down. Smiling wryly, the waitress refilled the glass. Slender and hard-looking, her wrinkles had wrinkles.

"What can I get you, hon?"

It occurred to Bethany that she hadn't eaten all day. That couldn't be good for the baby. Her cramp easing, Bethany heard the door open behind her as she glanced at the menu on the wall. "What's the bean burger?"

"A joke. And a bad one. Ain't nobody ordered one of them things since I been here, and I been here since the doors opened. You one of them vegetarians, are you?"

"Uh, no."

"Regular burger, then?"

"Sure. No fries."

The waitress, whose name tag identified her as Shug, yelled over her shoulder, "One favorite, minus the spuds!" She immediately turned a smile upward, looking past Bethany. "Well, hello, sugar. Make yourself at home."

"Thanks," said a man's deep voice.

Boots clumped on the floor, then the cowboy from the parking lot slid onto a stool to Bethany's right, placing his hat, brim up, on the vacant seat between them. The waitress plunked down another glass of water and leaned on the counter. "You look like a hungry man. What'll you have?"

He waved a big, long-fingered hand. Bethany noticed from the corner of her eye that his hair was blond with a touch of tawny red to it. She looked away as he turned his head toward her.

"I'll have the favorite, with the fries," he said in that deep, slightly amused voice. "To go. And the biggest iced tea you can manage."

"A favorite with the works!" Shug shouted, reaching for a forty-four-ounce disposable cup.

Bethany shook her head, remembering fondly the days when she could have downed the same without thinking about it. She'd spend all day trotting to the bathroom if she tried that now. The waitress delivered the iced tea, flirting mildly all the while, before turning back to Bethany.

"Anything to drink 'cept water for you, hon?"

"The water's fine. I was told that I could get a bus ticket here, though."

"Yes, ma'am." Shug stuck her pencil into the wild bun atop her head and reached under the counter, coming up with a big, hardbound book. "Where you headed, hon?"

"Buffalo Creek."

Beside her, the tall cowboy shifted, as if his interest had been stirred.

Shug consulted some sort of schedule and shook her head. "The nine-twenty-two goes right past there, but it don't stop 'til Dallas. Gets in there around midnight."

Dallas. "You've got to be kidding me," Bethany murmured, dropping her forehead into her upturned palm. That was at least forty miles too far, and how was she to get back to Buffalo Creek? Garrett had written that he'd bought a used motorcycle for transportation. Even if they could somehow manage her luggage, she wasn't stupid enough to climb onto the back of that in her condition. Besides, he had no idea that she was coming—or even that she was pregnant.

"You wouldn't know how much a taxi might cost from Dallas to Buffalo Creek, would you?" she asked Shug.

"Honey," the other woman said drily, "this right here is as close as I've ever been to either place. Or anywhere else for that matter."

"I see." Gulping, Bethany swept a hand over her bulging stomach.

"Well, you think on it," Shug said, stowing the book again. "You got nearly five hours before that bus gets here."

Bethany suppressed a sigh and offered up a wan smile. God, as usual, did not seem to be listening to her. Someone else clearly was, though.

"Did I hear someone mention Buffalo Creek?" the cowboy interjected, swiveling on his stool.

Shug immediately drifted his way, saying, "Little mama here is trying to get there. You know it?"

"Yep," he said. "Headed that direction myself."

Bethany finally turned to look at him. She didn't generally find light-haired men attractive, but this was a shockingly handsome man with smiling, cinnamon-brown eyes and dimples that cut grooves into his lean cheeks and a made a cleft in his strong, square chin. His neatly sculpted lips curled up at the corners, a lock of tawny hair falling rakishly across a high brow.

His gaze dropped to her protruding belly, then slid to the luggage stacked beside her. He turned away the next moment, but then he seemed to make a decision.

"I can give you a ride, if you like."

"There you go!" Shug crowed, throwing a hand at Bethany even as she addressed the cowboy. "I knew you was a gentleman."

The cowboy winked at her, and she laughed. The woman must live to flirt. "What do you think, hon?" she asked Bethany. "This your lucky day or what?"

"Oh. Uh…" Bethany stalled, waiting for the alarms to go off in her brain. Everyone knew that accepting rides from strangers was a dangerous proposition. Even if she was hopelessly stranded. She shook her head. "Th-that's very kind, but I wouldn't want to impose."

"No imposition," he said, "and I don't blame you for being wary. I just thought…" He shrugged, propped his elbows on the counter and turned his head to look at her. "You seem to be traveling alone."

Bethany lifted her chin. "I am."

"The Dallas bus station is right downtown," he went on, nodding. "I wouldn't want anyone I know stepping down there alone at midnight with no idea how to get where she needs to go next."

Bethany gulped. "I see."

A bell dinged. Shug whirled away and back again, sliding a plate onto the counter in front of Bethany.

"Want I should write down his tag number and take a picture of him with my cell phone?" she asked. "Just in case he ain't the gentleman he sizes up to be." She grinned at the cowboy, adding, "Just 'cause you're good-looking don't mean a girl hadn't ought to protect herself. In fact, it probably means she should!"

He chuckled. "Hey, I'm harmless, just trying to do a good turn." He reached into his back pocket and pulled out his wallet. "You can take a photo of my driver's license if that makes everyone feel better."

"That'd come in handy in case I feel the need to call the law," Shug said bluntly, pulling her phone out of her apron pocket.

He slapped his license onto the counter, and Shug took a photo of it.

"How about your phone number, too? In case I feel the need to call *you*." She waggled her eyebrows. "Maybe I need a ride to Buffalo Creek."

He laughed, and that bell dinged again. A white sack appeared in the kitchen window, and the cowboy got to his feet, reaching for his license as Shug carried the sack to the cash register.

"Better make up your mind," he said to Bethany, "because I can't leave those horses sitting out there in the heat any longer." He looked down at her then, saying, "I'm harmless, I promise, but it's up to you."

Suddenly, she remembered what she'd been doing when she'd first caught sight of his rig. She'd been praying for a safe way to get to her brother, with a minimum of delay and hassle. Maybe, she thought, God *had* actually listened this time.

"I ought to call first and let someone know I'm coming."

"Go ahead."

Making her decision, she got to her feet. "Ma'am, Shug, could I use your phone?"

"Why, sure, hon." The waitress handed it over, reaching for Bethany's untouched plate with the other hand. "I'll just wrap this up for you."

The cowboy put out his hand. "Name's Chandler."

"Bethany," she said, placing her hand in his. "Bethany Ca—" She stumbled over the surname. "Willows. Bethany Willows." She still couldn't help thinking of herself as Bethany Carter. That, however, was behind her now, and all that really mattered was getting to Garrett and finding a way to make a life for herself and her child.

Stepping away, she called for the first time the cell-phone number that Garrett had sent in his letter. She had not dared call before, with all that had been going on in her life and his, and she dared not bring it up now, for both their sakes.

After only a few seconds, he answered. Relieved to hear the sound of her beloved brother's voice, she mentioned tentatively that she was coming to see him. He sounded elated and assured her that it would be no problem. She almost told him about the cowboy, but in the end, she decided against it.

Why worry him when he could do nothing about it, having only a motorcycle as transportation and a workday to get through? She wouldn't impose on him too much or jeopardize the life he'd managed to put together for himself. Besides, she felt no threat from this Mr. Chandler. Maybe it was because he was so handsome, but if he'd meant her ill, why would he have let Shug take a photo of his license? Garrett, however, wasn't likely to see it that way. Prison, she had heard, made a man suspicious.

Getting off the phone as quickly as she could, she passed

it back to its owner, smiled her thanks and squared her shoulders before facing the stranger who had offered her a ride.

"I'm ready."

"Let's get on the road. Next stop Buffalo Creek."

"Uh, no," she muttered, patting her belly, "I think we'll be stopping before then."

He just laughed and pointed her out the door.

Biting off a huge chunk of burger, Chandler chewed a few times and swallowed without ever taking his eyes off the road. He'd already made short work of the fries, preferring to eat them while they were hot.

"I guess Shug was right," his passenger commented. "You were a hungry man."

"Not really."

He glanced in Bethany's direction and again felt the jolt of her beauty. God had blessed this Bethany Willows with sleek brown-black hair, pale pink skin as smooth as porcelain and a startlingly piquant face. Broad at the brow and cheek but with an adorably pointed chin, it put him in mind of a drawing of a fairy princess in a children's book. Her delicate nose and brows offset huge, tilted eyes of cornflower blue, rimmed with dark lashes, and wide, plump lips of a rich, dusky rose.

She shifted in her seat, crossing her legs beneath the full skirt of her flower-print sundress. The straps of the elasticized bodice tied at the shoulders, emphasizing the delicate line of her collarbone. She seemed petite but was, in fact, taller than average. He judged her to stand at least seven inches over five feet, which still left her a good eight inches shorter than his own six-foot-three-inch height. The pregnancy bump merely called attention to her long, slender limbs and lithe dancer's body.

"So you stopped to eat but you weren't hungry?" Those

big blue eyes looked a question at him, her fairy face tilting to one side.

He tried hard to marshal his thoughts. Aiming his gaze straight ahead, he formulated an explanation. "When you rodeo for a living, you learn to eat on the move and whenever it's convenient. I saw a good place to park the trailer, it was getting on to the dinner hour, so I pulled over."

A big part of what he did for a living was just getting him, his horses and his gear from one place to the next. It was a logistical nightmare sometimes, and took careful planning. He and his partner, Pat Kreger, sat down every few weeks and worked out a schedule, deciding which contests made the most sense. They'd managed to improve their standings year by year and had hoped that this year they might make the national finals in team roping, which was why Chandler was alarmed and somewhat irritated by Kreger's failure to show up in Georgia this past weekend.

The Fourth of July holiday offered up some of the richest rodeos of the summer, and Kreger should have been there, but he hadn't showed, and his phone went straight to voice mail every time Chandler called. No one Chandler had spoken to had any idea where Kreger might be, and that was decidedly odd, for Pat was a particularly sociable fellow. Chandler supposed that his partner could be ill and holed up in the little house they shared on the small ranch that they co-owned, but it was more likely that he'd merely given in to some wild impulse and hared off in a different direction. It had happened before, though not often.

If his sister Kaylie, a nurse, had been in town instead of gallivanting around Europe on her honeymoon, Chandler would have asked her to go out to the ranch and check. As it was, he could only hope and pray that Kreger was well and could offer up some clever excuse.

"So you're a rodeo cowboy, are you?" Bethany Willows asked, pulling his thoughts back to the moment.

"That's right."

"What events?"

"Tie-down roping, steer wrestling, team roping."

"No bull riding or bronc busting?"

Chandler grimaced mentally. Those were the glamorous events. Bull riders and bronc busters were tough, skillful *hombres,* but the most successful ones were compact men with low centers of gravity. Chandler's size and skill set partly dictated the events in which he competed, but he wouldn't have had it any other way. He loved working with a rope. Still, he wanted to impress this woman, silly as that seemed.

"Nope, and no barrel racing, either," he answered flippantly.

She laughed at that, barrel racing usually being a female event, and he cut her a glance that became a stare when he caught sight of that beaming smile. It knocked the breath right out of him and left his chest hurting. He stared until she lifted her burger in both hands and nipped off a small bite with her even, white teeth. Freshly jolted, he jerked his gaze back to the highway and gobbled down the last of his own meal. Wadding up the wrapper, he dropped the paper into the bag standing open on the console between the seats, doing his best to forget what he'd seen. Or rather, what he had not seen.

He had not seen a wedding ring on her long, tapered, slender finger.

Chapter Two

"So where can I drop you?" the cowboy asked, carefully checking both of his sideview mirrors as he clicked on the rig's right signal.

They had driven in silence for the better part of the trip, though he had stopped when she'd asked him to, without complaint. The silence had been protracted during this last leg of the journey, however, so much so that Bethany had closed her eyes and pretended to sleep for part of the time. Now, she waited to reply until the truck and trailer had exited the highway.

She gave him the address. He gaped at her, his reddish-brown eyes popping wide.

"That's Chatam House!"

"Yes, do you know it?"

He studied her as if trying to decide whether she was serious. "How do *you* know it?"

"Oh, I grew up around here," she answered airily, not about to tell him the whole of that story.

He gave her an odd look. "That makes two of us. Actually, I still live here, and I almost always have, except for when I was away at college. I have a little ranch out west of town now."

"I left Buffalo Creek as soon as I graduated high school," she said. She had literally walked out of the graduation ceremony, gotten into Jay Carter's car and driven straight to the airport, where they'd hopped on a plane to Vegas. Two days later, he'd carried her over the threshold of the house in Humble and left her there while he raced off on business.

"That's probably part of it," the cowboy mused. "What year was that?"

She told him, and he nodded. "I graduated from college that same year. That would make you about twenty-four. Right?"

"Exactly twenty-four."

"I'm twenty-nine. Guess we just moved in different circles back then. My sister Kaylie's about your age, though."

Bethany shook her head, trying to remember any Chandlers she might have known. "I don't recall her." That wasn't surprising. She hadn't had many friends. Her stepfather hadn't liked anyone coming around the house to witness his abusive behavior.

"I guess Buffalo Creek's not as small as it feels sometimes," Chandler murmured.

"What is it, about thirty thousand people now?"

"Something like that," he said, nodding. He made a careful left turn and eased over a pair of railroad tracks.

Those old tracks, leftover from the days when Buffalo Creek had been a major transportation center for the cotton growers in the area, crisscrossed the town. The cotton was long gone now, but the trains still rattled through town several times a day. Oddly enough, Bethany had missed them when she'd first moved to Humble. The trains were all she had missed, though. Garrett had already been sent to prison, and their mother had been a different person by then. After their mother's death, Bethany would never have considered coming back if Garrett had not returned here. She still didn't understand why he had, really. Maybe the parole board had dictated where he had to go.

As the city rolled past, one graceful street after another, excitement built in Bethany. Her hands skimmed over her belly. Her pregnancy was going to be a shock to Garrett. She probably should have told him, but they'd been out of touch when she'd first realized that she was pregnant. He'd just gotten out of prison, and she'd had no idea where he was headed or how to reach him. Then her world had begun to dissolve, and she'd judged it wiser, all things considered, not to tell her brother about it.

She'd never dreamed how it would all turn out. How could she?

Obviously, Chandler mused, he needed a refresher course in the basics of introductions. Somehow, he hadn't managed to get his last name out there at the diner, and Bethany had apparently assumed that his given name was his surname. Or had she? He tried to remember if she had glanced at his driver's license as it had lain there on the counter, but he just didn't know.

Thinking of that bare ring finger on her left hand, Chandler took his eyes off the road long enough to glance at her pretty face, and a shiver of *something* crawled right up his spine to the top of his head.

What, he had to ask himself, were the odds that he'd just accidentally run into a pregnant stranger on the side of the road who was headed not only for his hometown of Buffalo Creek, Texas, but right to his family home? The aunties, no doubt, had something to do with this.

His aunts, maiden triplets in their seventies, might be a tad on the eccentric side, but they were good women. Even more than his retired minister father, they epitomized Christianity for Chandler. They lived to serve a greater cause, dedicating their time, talent, money and even their home, the antebellum mansion known as Chatam House, to the needs of others. They weren't perfect, of course.

Hypatia, the undisputed head of the household, could be a bit prim. She wore her dignity, along with her pearls, like a protective cloak. Magnolia, or Mags, on the other hand, couldn't have been any more down-to-earth if she was covered in it, which she often was, being a master gardener much more concerned with the appearance of her roses than herself. It wasn't unusual, in fact, to find Aunt Mags in a dress and rubber boots decorated with mud. Odelia, bless her, was sweetness personified, sweetness with a heavy dose of silliness. He, along with his cousins, secretly but fondly referred to her as Auntie Od and chuckled about the weird clothing and oversize jewelry that she wore. She especially had a thing for earrings and lace hankies, so much so that the rest of the family routinely speculated about how many of each she might actually possess.

Chandler smiled. No, not perfect but very dear, and as generous and loving as it was possible for three human beings to be. Why, last winter they'd opened their home to his cousin Reeves and Reeves's little girl, Gillian, and just recently, they'd taken in an injured professional hockey player, who just happened to be Chandler's new brother-in-law. Yes, whatever had brought pretty, pregnant Bethany Willows here to Chatam House, the aunties almost surely had a hand in it. He supposed he'd find out what that was soon, as they had just passed the brick column at the eastern edge of the fifteen-acre estate.

He slowed the rig, braking carefully so as not to stress the quartet of horses riding in the trailer. Those animals, each one trained to a specific task, were essential to his livelihood and constituted a significant financial investment, besides being as dear to him as any pet. As the rig slowed, Bethany sat up very straight, her hands clasping her belly, her gaze trained out the window at the shoulder-high yew hedge that flanked the wrought-iron fence.

They came to the gate, which stood open, as usual, its elaborate scrolls and bars culminating in a large, brass-plated *C,* and there, on a slight rise, stood the grand old house. Two stories of whitewashed, hand-hewn stone blocks, it featured half a dozen Doric columns across the veranda and a substantial porte cochere on the west end. The black trim around the windows and doors echoed the color of the black slate roof, just as the redbrick walkways and steps, flanked by a colorful profusion of flowers, reflected that of the tall chimneys. Dead center of the veranda stood a bright yellow door framed by narrow, leaded-glass windows on the sides and an elaborate fan-shaped one on top.

Chandler eased the rig between the brick gate columns and aimed it up the deeply graveled drive that swept over the easy, green-blanketed hill and circled back onto itself, branching off at the top to pass beneath the porte cochere and on past the carriage house, erected at right angles behind the mansion. The staff, Chester and Hilda Worth and Hilda's sister Carol Petty, lived in rooms above the carriage house bays, as did Magnolia's mysterious new gardener, Garrett somebody.

Garrett, a tall, dark-haired man in jeans and a snugly fitted T-shirt, strode across the lawn at that very moment, apparently heading toward the enormous old magnolia tree on the west lawn. Bethany swiftly released her safety belt with one hand and slapped the button to roll down the window with the other.

"Garrett! Garrett!"

Her hands fumbled for the door handle and the lock. Alarmed, Chandler braked to a stop. She grabbed her handbag and literally baled out, sobbing and laughing.

"Garrett!"

The muscular, dark-haired man lifted a hand to shade his

eyes from the sun as he looked in her direction, then he took off running toward her. Just before he got there, she turned to hold out a hand, yelling to Chandler, "Wait! Just wait!"

Garrett Whatever-His-Last-Name-Was threw his arms around Bethany, lifting her off her feet. The pair embraced tightly for several moments, so wrapped up in each other that they didn't have eyes for anyone or anything else, their dark heads bent close. Chandler put the truck in Park, set the brake and got out. Still the two clung together.

Not quite able to look away from what he knew to be a very emotionally charged moment, Chandler pulled Bethany's luggage from the backseat of the truck and set it on the brick walkway before ambling toward the house. He'd reached the steps up to the porch before Garrett the gardener set Bethany back on her feet, his hands going to her distended belly. Chandler saw Bethany duck her head and had the distinct impression that Garrett hadn't known about the child. He did not look displeased, however, just the opposite. In fact, he and Bethany seemed to care deeply for each other.

Shaking his head wryly, Chandler stepped up into the shadows of the deep veranda. Looked like the aunties' new gardener had a family in the making. Chandler was more than a little envious. One day he would like to have a beautiful wife like her and a couple kids. But first, he had to get his financial house in order.

If he and Kreger continued to finish in the money for the rest of the year, Chandler could finally pay off his share of the ranch and think about building his own house on the place. That would leave Pat in full possession of his childhood home and allow both of them to start new phases in their lives. Right now, though, that gardener out there was in a better position to support a wife and child than Chandler was.

Not bothering to knock or ring the bell, he did what most

of the family would do; he opened the door and walked in, knowing well that the house was rarely locked until the last person retired for the night. He'd been in that marble-floored foyer a thousand times, but still he measured with his eyes the sweep of the magnificent staircase that curved up to the second floor and lifted his gaze past the sparkling chandelier to the ceiling, where some unknown artist had painted blue sky, gauzy clouds and wafting white feathers. He'd never understand how that person had managed to give the impression of sunshine and magnificence. It left the viewer with the feeling that God looked down from Heaven upon the Chatam household. Chandler had always found that a particularly comforting thought, almost as comforting as the aunties themselves, whom he was suddenly anxious to see.

"Hello!" he called. "Where is everyone?"

A frothy white head appeared around the edge of the library door on his right. It was topped by a big, floppy bow of pale pink and anchored by big, butterfly-shaped earrings colored in variegated shades of pink, purple, yellow and blue. A bright pink smile broke across a rounded, drooping face with the Chatam cleft chin. Amber eyes twinkling, Odelia stepped into the foyer in a swirl of multicolored gossamer layers.

"Chandler, dear! There you are!"

The ubiquitous lace hanky appeared, beckoning him to follow. Smiling broadly, he strolled into what was one of his very favorite rooms in the big old house, but he didn't get far, his way blocked by a head-high stack of cardboard boxes.

Hypatia came from behind the stack to kiss his cheek, her silver hair twisted into a smooth figure eight at the nape of her slender neck, pearls in place. She wore a crisp, collarless, linen suit of khaki tan with elbow-length sleeves and a pleated skirt.

"We've been expecting you," she said in indulgent tones.

"Expecting me?" He remembered suddenly that Bethany had called ahead. No, that couldn't be right. Bethany hadn't known who he was, so she wouldn't have told Garrett to expect him, Chandler Chatam, to be with her, and even if she had, it wasn't as if he and the gardener had ever officially met. He'd only glimpsed the man from a distance and heard him mentioned. Chandler shifted his weight, one booted foot placed forward, his hands at his belt. "What do you mean, you were expecting me?"

"Well, when that nice Mr. Kreger dropped off your things for you," Odelia trilled, "he said you'd be along." She waved her hanky at the stack of boxes.

Shock rolled over Chandler in waves. "Kreger, P-Pat Kreger, brought this stuff over here?"

"Just a little while ago," Hypatia confirmed.

Chandler thumped himself in the chest, asking stupidly, "For me?"

"Of course, dear," Hypatia said. "We hung your clothing in the cloakroom until you decide which suite you want."

Chandler turned around and walked out into the foyer again. He stalked past the staircase and partway down what was referred to as the "east" hall to the first door on the left. Chandler opened the door and stepped inside the cluttered space. There, along one wall, hung a dozen pairs of neatly pressed jeans and almost twice that many shirts, all his.

Shock morphed into a confused, unwieldy amalgamation of emotions, the only one he could identify being anger. Whirling, he stepped back into the hall. And nearly bowled over Mags. She shoved her thick, iron-gray braid off her shoulder and folded her arms, making the short sleeves of her dark plaid, shirtwaist dress cut into her surprisingly pronounced biceps. She looked up at him, a frown on her wrinkled, work-hewn face, her cleft chin thrust forward mulishly.

"What's going on, Chandler?" she demanded.

"I don't...I..."

Her expression softened, and she clamped a spotted, surprisingly strong hand onto his forearm. "You can tell us, dear," she said. "Obviously, since you had Kreger bring your things here, you know we'll help in any way we can, though hopefully it won't mean choosing sides between you and your father."

His father. Chandler pushed away any consideration of that situation and focused on the part that had to do with his supposed partner.

"I'm sorry, Aunt Mags, but I have to find Kreger." He looked past her toward the foyer, determination hardening his jaw. "Right now."

He sidestepped around her and strode to the front door, which he went through without a word of farewell. Whatever Kreger was up to, Chandler told himself, the explanation had better be a good one. He saw nothing of Bethany and the gardener, but at the moment his thoughts were centered on his own problems. Bethany Willows and Garrett could take care of themselves.

The rumble of the engine preceded the sound of tires on gravel by less than two seconds. Bethany rose from her seat on the brick steps at the side of the house beneath the carport, or porte cochere, as Garrett called it, and hurried toward the front drive. She arrived just in time to see Chandler's rig completing the loop as it headed for the street. She glanced to the side and saw that her luggage waited for her on the front walk. The truck turned right onto the street and accelerated. Unaccountably deflated, Bethany sighed.

"Guess he got tired of waiting." She turned back and retraced her steps, dragging her toes in the gravel.

"Is that a problem?" Garrett asked. "You said he's not your husband."

"I said I don't have a husband," Bethany corrected softly.

"Actually," Garrett pointed out, his gaze skimming over her distended belly, "I think you said that you've *never* had a husband."

Bethany stepped up next to him, turned and sat on the rough edge of the brick. "That's right." She repositioned her handbag on the step, keeping her gaze averted.

"So when you wrote me to say you'd eloped to Las Vegas…" Garrett prodded.

"Wasn't true," she admitted tersely, propping her elbows on her knees and resting her chin in the cradle of her upturned palms. She'd only thought it true at the time, but Garrett didn't need to know that. No one did.

"And this Jay Carter?"

"Never existed." True again, as far as it went.

"Then why," Garrett demanded, spreading his hands, "did you let me believe all this time that he did?"

Bethany bowed her head, debating with herself. If she told Garrett the truth, he'd want to go after Jay, just the way he'd gone after their stepfather for hurting their mom; yet, she couldn't quite bring herself to outright lie to him. Closing her eyes, she whispered another part of the truth, "I didn't want you to worry about me."

When she turned her head, she found his piercing blue gaze trained on her from beneath his dark brows. He shoved both hands through his dark, spiky hair. Like her, he had a bit of a pointed chin, but his strong, square jaw was perpetually shadowed with the soot of a heavy beard that he'd struggled to keep cleanly shaved since the age of fourteen. At six-one, e wasn't as tall as the cowboy, she mused, but Garrett was a bit more bulky. He'd muscled up in prison, but he'd always been stronger than average and of a protective nature.

"If I hadn't been in prison, you wouldn't have had to lie to me," he muttered.

Bethany groaned, feeling lower than dirt. "You've got to be kidding! My situation is not your fault. How could you even think it?"

Garrett came up off the steps. Whirling to face her, he thumped himself in the chest. "I was the one in prison! I should have been here for you—and Mom."

Bethany stood and went to him, placing her hands on the hard bulges of his biceps. "You went to prison because you tried to help Mom."

Their father had died in a ditch collapse when Garrett was seven years old and Bethany four. Ten years later their mom, Shirley, had remarried. Doyle turned out to be a controlling, abusive brute who regularly beat their mother. Three years into the marriage, he had beat Shirley so severely that she'd been hospitalized for nearly a week. The day that Doyle had gotten out of jail on bail, Garrett had gone after him, giving the brute a taste of his own medicine. The result had been Garrett's own arrest. Unable to make his bail for himself, Garrett had languished in jail for several months. During that time, Doyle convinced Shirley to forgive him and drop all charges. In frustration, Garrett had pleaded guilty to a reduced charge and gone to prison, telling Bethany that they were all better off that way, for Doyle would surely beat Shirley again and it would be safer if Garrett couldn't get his hands on the man. He was too right. Not two years later, Doyle had beat their mother to death.

"That doesn't change the fact that I wasn't here for you," Garrett insisted.

"You couldn't help Mom or me," Bethany insisted, "and

I'm glad you were out of it." She had escaped herself as soon as she could. Pushing away thoughts of the past, she looked to her brother. "I'm so glad to be with you again."

He hugged her. "Ditto." After a moment, he went on nonchalantly, "So, is the cowboy the baby's father?"

Stunned, Bethany pulled back. Denial leaped to the tip of her tongue, but for some reason she clamped her lips against it. Maybe because she wished the cowboy was the father. At least he was kind to her and true to his word. Better him than a scheming liar and cheat. Besides, it was best to say nothing at all about the baby's father.

"Tell and I'll take that kid you want so much. Don't think I can't."

Shivering, she said, "It doesn't matter who the father is. This is my baby, mine alone."

"Why'd you break up with him?"

She looked down at her toes. "He doesn't want to be a father."

Garrett shifted his weight, his feet scuffing in the gravel. "That why you came here, Bethy?" he asked, using her childhood nickname.

She turned back to him, her eyes filling with tears. "I came because I wanted to see you, and because I didn't have anywhere else to go. I don't have enough money to get my own place or any way to pay the rent just now. I hoped you'd be able to help us out until the baby comes."

Nodding, he asked, "When is that?"

"Middle of October."

"So about three and a half months."

"Yes."

"I think we can work out something." He slipped an arm about her shoulders and walked her across the redbrick stoop and through a bright yellow door into a long, dark hallway.

"The misses will probably be in the front parlor waiting

or dinner," he told her. They walked on to the end of the
hall past a TV room on one side and a kitchen on the other,
according to the aromas emanating from that room. "Food's
great here," Garrett told her with a smile. "This is the west
hall," Garrett informed her as they turned right. "There's
a real ballroom off the east hall, along with a music room,
library and study. Dining room's on this side." He waved a
hand.

They came to the end of a broad, sweeping staircase
in what was obviously the front foyer of the house. They
stopped, and Garrett turned his gaze upward, pointing
toward the ceiling. Bethany gasped at the mural overhead
and took in the sparkling crystal chandelier. Garrett ushered
her through the wide door of a large room crammed with
antiques and flowers.

An older woman rose from an armchair placed at a right
angle to them. Short and sturdy, she wore a dark shirtwaist
dress with penny loafers. Her gray hair hung across one
shoulder in a thick braid, the tip brushing a pair of reading
glasses in her breast pocket. Her oval face, while wrinkled
and sagging a bit, showed a lean strength. She regarded
Bethany with bright amber eyes, tilting her cleft chin to one
side.

"Hello," she said, curiosity ringing in her voice.

"Bethany," Garrett said, "I'd like to introduce you to Miss
Magnolia Faye Chatam. Miss Magnolia, this is my sister."

"Oh, my dear!" Magnolia exclaimed. "What a surprise!"
She hurried forward, reaching out for Bethany's hand and
clasping it firmly. "You are as pretty as your brother is handsome."

Bethany smiled. "Thank you. He says you've been very
kind to him."

Magnolia waved that away. "He's been a great help to me."

"Ma'am, I already owe y'all more than I can ever repay,"

Garrett said solemnly, "but I hope you don't mind if I ask a favor of you. My sister needs a place to stay. I'd like her to stay with me for a while, if you and the other misses don't mind."

Magnolia seemed slightly taken aback. "In that tiny attic room?"

"We can manage," Garrett insisted. He clasped a hand onto Bethany's shoulder. "She doesn't have anywhere else to go, ma'am."

Two new heads popped up then, and two more pairs of amber eyes turned Bethany's way. Another woman rose from another wing chair. She turned fully to face them, her manner almost regal. Despite her leaner, paler face, she looked very like Magnolia, her silver hair coiled in a heavy, figure-eight chignon at the nape of her neck. Her collarless tan suit called attention to the strand of pearls at her throat, and she held in one hand a pair of gold-rimmed half-glasses.

The third sister wore a flutter of rainbow organza. Plumper than the other two, she wore her stark white hair in short, fluffy curls with a big, floppy, soft pink bow tied atop her head and a pair of large, brightly colored organza butterflies affixed to her earlobes. It was all Bethany could do not to laugh with delight.

Tearing her gaze away from the butterfly lady, Bethany looked to Magnolia.

"My sisters," she said. "Miss Odelia Mae Chatam and Miss Hypatia Kay Chatam." Bethany nodded at each in turn.

"Sisters," Magnolia said, "I have the privilege of introducing Garrett's sister, Bethany…" Her voice trailed off.

The moment of truth had arrived, the moment when they would know what a fool she had been. Would they look down on her? Would they judge? She gulped and lifted her chin.

"Bethany Sue. Bethany Sue Willows."

Not a Mrs. Nor a miss. Just Bethany Sue Willows. And more pain and shame than she knew how to bear.

Chapter Three

The sisters traded looks.

"Ms. Willows," Hypatia said, inclining her head. "Welcome to Chatam House."

Bethany nearly collapsed with relief. "Thank you, but won't you please call me Bethany?"

Hypatia Chatam smiled serenely. "Thank you. Given names are always easier with three Miss Chatams about." She beckoned them closer with a wave of one hand, saying, "Join us, please."

Magnolia crossed over and took a seat next to Odelia on an elaborately carved settee upholstered in a lush floral damask. Hypatia returned to the gold-striped wingback and nodded Bethany toward its twin. Garrett stood beside her, his arm stretched across the chair back.

"When is the baby due?" Odelia warbled eagerly, butterflies dancing.

"Eighteenth of October," Bethany answered cautiously.

"So," Magnolia said to her sisters, "the master suite, do you think?"

"What?" Garrett exclaimed. "No, no, that's not necessary."

They blithely ignored him.

"Hmm, yes, I think that would be best," Hypatia mused.

Odelia clapped her hands again. "Room for the two of you and the baby!"

Without warning, Bethany burst into tears. "I'm sorry! Garrett said you were kind, but I never dreamed...I never expected..."

"Now, now," Hypatia said calmly.

"It has become clear to us," Magnolia put in, "that the good Lord has ordained Chatam House as a place of sanctuary for those in need. We are only following His dictates, dear."

"And babies are such fun!" Odelia chirruped.

Bethany laughed, blinking away her tears. "I don't know how to thank you. I promise I won't abuse your hospitality. I intend to look for a job right away."

"Is that wise in your condition?" Odelia worried aloud.

"I was working until I came here," Bethany told her staunchly. "I can certainly continue."

"That might not be so easy," Garrett warned. "It's one thing to continue working at a job after you become pregnant. It's another to get someone to hire you when you're almost six months along."

"Well, it's a matter for prayer," Hypatia said in a tone that clearly indicated the subject was closed for the moment. "Bethany, I'm sure you'd like to freshen up before dinner. Garrett, will you show her the retiring room, then ask Carol to set two extra places at the dining table."

Garrett nodded. "I'll get your bags in, too, sis."

"Chester will help you both settle into your new space later," Hypatia decreed.

"Father would be so tickled, don't you think?" Odelia said as Bethany rose and hurried from the room at Garrett's side.

"The master suite was old Mr. Chatam's room," Garrett whispered to Bethany. "He died at the age of ninety-two in nineteen-ninety-nine, and they still speak as if it was yesterday."

"I don't care if they set a place for him at the dinner table!" Bethany whispered back.

"They're not *that* eccentric, and they're sharp as razors, believe me."

"Oh, Garrett," Bethany cried, laying her head on his shoulder, "I'm so glad I came!"

Maybe, she told herself, the Willows family was finally going to come right.

"Well, my dears," Hypatia said, keeping her voice low, "it looks as though we're going to have a full house."

Magnolia nodded, oddly satisfied. She'd known Garrett as a child. After his father had died, Garrett had come around occasionally asking to mow the yard. She'd let him mow for an hour or so, paid him and sent him on his way. After his mother had remarried, he'd started showing up with bruises, but he would never answer Magnolia's questions about how he'd obtained them. She'd heard rumors, but once she'd asked outright if his stepfather had hit him, Garrett had stopped visiting. Later, when she'd learned that Mrs. Benjamin had been hospitalized and Garrett had assaulted his stepfather, she'd expected the boy to get off with a reprimand. Instead, he'd gone to prison. She had always considered that a grave miscarriage of justice, so when he had approached her in the yard just over two months ago, Magnolia had hired him on the spot. Garrett had quickly become a household favorite. Now, his pregnant sister, Bethany, had come to them. Magnolia definitely felt the hand of God at work.

"Even with Chandler here," she said, "I don't see what else we could have done."

"Oh, of course Bethany has to stay!" Odelia gushed. She

bit her lip. "But I know I heard Kaylie say that Garrett's sister was married."

Hypatia nodded. "Yes. I recall the same thing."

"Perhaps they've divorced," Magnolia suggested.

"Perhaps," Hypatia murmured. "I confess to some curiosity, but all will undoubtedly become clear in time."

"What God wishes us to know, He will reveal," Magnolia added with a nod.

"I'm more concerned about Chandler, frankly," Hypatia went on.

Magnolia, too, was concerned about their nephew. They had hoped at first that his moving in here had signaled a compromise of sorts with his father, who disapproved of both Chandler's occupation and his partner, Kreger, but something else was obviously afoot, and Chandler hadn't seemed to know what that was.

"We've prayed a long time for him to make certain things right in his life," Magnolia pointed out. "Maybe the good Lord is forcing his hand a bit."

"True," Hypatia agreed.

"Or," Odelia exclaimed, hunching her shoulders with excitement, "we could have another romance brewing! Wouldn't that be lovely? Chandler and Bethany and a baby! What fun that would be!"

Magnolia rolled her eyes at her sister. "That's a stretch."

"Why? Don't you think she'll like Chandler?"

"That's not the point."

"I'm sure he'll like her, and they'll be living in the same house, after all. Once they get to know each other, anything could happen."

"Now, now," Hypatia cautioned sternly, holding up a hand. "We're getting just a bit carried away here, don't you think?"

Odelia turned a vexed gaze on her. "You're the one who always says that God has a reason for everything."

"Those reasons don't have to be romantic, though," Magnolia interjected.

Odelia blinked. "But they could be."

Hypatia sighed. "Let us leave this subject, please. We don't want to be assigning motives to God now, do we?"

"I suppose not," Odelia mumbled. Then she brightened. "But it will still be fun to have a baby in the house. Maybe we can babysit!"

Nodding, Magnolia shared a look with Hypatia, whose lips firmed against obvious laughter. Bowing her head to hide her own smile, Magnolia rolled her eyes again. Oh, to be as joyful as her dear, frothy-headed sister! On the other hand, Mags was supremely satisfied with her own life. The lives of her and her sisters had been, from the shared day of their birth, a life of privilege, which just meant, as Mama and Daddy had always said, that they were obliged by God to do as much good as they possibly could for others.

Lately, God seemed to be bringing those opportunities to do good right to their doorstep. The outcome thus far had been quite rewarding, resulting in two weddings.

While a romance seemed unlikely in this case, whatever God had in mind, Magnolia was sure that it would be, at the least, very interesting.

Sighing wearily, Chandler turned the rig between the gate-posts and aimed it up the rise toward Chatam House. He'd spent the last thirty-six hours fruitlessly trying to catch up with his old buddy and erstwhile partner, Patrick Kreger.

His very first course of action had been to drive straight out to the ranch, where he'd found a family by the name of Cantu in residence. Mr. Cantu had proudly claimed to have purchased the ranch only days earlier. A broken-down old piebald had snuffled around the corral next to the barn, the corral where Chandler had intended to off-load his own horses. Instead, after examining the loan closing papers that Cantu had graciously provided and recognizing Kreger's signature, Chandler had turned around and hit the road again, managing to keep his temper in check until he was away.

After he'd calmed down, he'd made two phone calls. The first was to his cousin Asher, an attorney, who agreed to see him Monday morning. The second call went to an old friend, Dovey Crawlick, who ran a shoestring animal rescue operation a mile or so southeast of town. She had kindly given Chandler space for his horses at a more-than-reasonable rent and told him that she'd heard Kreger was staying in the Maypearl area.

After following rumors across the state, Chandler eventually wound up calling on Kreger's elderly great-uncle, from whom Pat had recently requested a large loan and been refused.

"Don't hold with gambling," the old man had said morosely, "but he said they'd break his legs if he didn't come up with the cash."

Chandler had to conclude that Kreger had sold the ranch to cover his gambling debts. That was when Chandler had given up the chase. He'd known, of course, that Kreger was apt to wager a bit here and there, but it hadn't seemed to be a serious problem. Until now.

In a foul mood, Chandler made his way back to Chatam House in the wee hours of the morning. He couldn't help thinking about Bethany. Had the aunties allowed her to move into the carriage house with Garrett? He rather doubted that, unless of course the two were married. If they weren't, they probably soon would be. Then he'd have to see her, them, on a daily basis. With everything that had gone wrong in his life lately, that seemed like adding insult to injury.

Not wanting to rouse the household, he decided to sleep in his truck. It would not be the first time that he'd sacked out in the backseat. He needed to hide his trailer, though. Dovey hadn't had room for it at her place, but the aunties would not appreciate having a dirty horse hauler parked within sight of the street. Moving mechanically, he backed the trailer through the porte cochere, past the carriage house and around the corner of the building out of sight.

After rolling down all the windows to take advantage of the slight breeze, he crawled into the back cab. He set aside his hat, tugged off his belt and boots and curled up on the seat, his head pillowed on his folded forearms. But peace proved elusive as his mind played restlessly over all he'd learned.

That Pat had sold the ranch out from under Chandler hurt, but the reason hurt just as much. He'd trusted Pat Kreger. He had defended Pat staunchly against his father for years. In the end, however, Hub had been proved right about Kreger, and eventually Chandler would have to deal with that. Just then, though, he was trying to wrap his mind around the fifty-thousand-plus dollars that he'd apparently poured down a bottomless hole.

The thought made him physically ill, his disappointment so deep that it was a constant ache. His whole future had just disappeared! Why hadn't he known that Pat was out of control? Why had he made so many excuses for his old buddy?

Feeling brainless and foolish, Chandler did the only thing he knew to do. He prayed.

Lord, I need Your help here, he began. *I've been stubborn and stupid and, boy, am I paying for it. I'll be paying for some time to come, too. But I deserve it. So I guess first of all I need to ask for Your forgiveness. I really want to do better from now on, to let You guide me. Meanwhile, I'm in a fix. I can't live off my old aunts. I need some real cash.*

To get that, I need a new partner, but how do I find a new partner when I'm not even sure I can trust my own judgment anymore? Please give me some real direction here, Lord.

Chandler went on, pouring out his troubles and concerns, facing his deepest fears and failures and beseeching his Lord for aid. He thought of Bethany again. By all appearances, things had turned out well for her, at least. He felt a prick of envy, but whether for her or Garrett, he didn't know. A little of both, maybe. He drifted into a place of comfort before he could figure it out, and rest found him at last. He slept deeply and completely, his mind a blank, despite the heat and cramped quarters.

Suddenly, bright daylight blinded him. He thought that he must be dreaming, for hands seemed to grapple about his shoulders. Fists closed in the fabric of his shirt, and he instinctively stiffened. The next instant he was being pulled bodily through the open window of the truck cab.

Panicked, he brought his feet up onto the seat and pushed, angling his shoulders through the window, until he could get his hands on the roof of the truck and haul out the rest of the way. He barely got a foot on the ground when a fist slammed into his shoulder. It would have hit his jaw if he hadn't been in the process of bringing down his second foot.

"Hey!"

He let the blow turn him, his hands coming up defensively, and glimpsed a dark head before a second fist flew his way. Ducking left, he felt knuckles clip his ear. Tucking his chin, Chandler threw a hard right, glancing a blow off his opponent's ribs. After an answering pop high on the left side of his chest, he started slugging madly. A savvy fighter, the other guy stepped in close, wrapped his arms around Chandler's shoulders and threw him onto the ground. Chandler made sure that they both went down, twisting to land on his side rather than his back.

"Can't leave her alone, can you?" a voice growled in his ear as the two wrestled.

"What?" Chandler squawked.

"You're not going to bounce in and out of her life!"

"Who?"

"Don't want the kid, but you want her, don't you?"

"What're you tal—"

Something hit Chandler on the side of the face and shoulder, something prickly and stiff.

"Ow!"

"Ouch!" yelped the other guy.

Chandler rolled away, becoming aware of a great din, something more than his own grunts and groans and the scrabble of gravel. One sound stood out among the others, the sound of his aunt's voice.

"Stop that! Stop it right now!"

Realizing that the blows had ceased, Chandler looked up. Magnolia glared down at him, a broom in her hands.

"Aunt Mags?"

"What on earth do you think you're doing, Chandler Chatam?"

"Defending myself!" Chandler exclaimed.

At the same time, his opponent barked, "Chatam?"

She switched her gaze in that direction. "And you, Garrett Willows! Why are you fighting with my nephew?"

Garrett rocketed to his feet. "He's your nephew?"

Chandler sat up, trying to catch his breath. Garrett the gardener had attacked him? He glared up at the dark-haired man towering uncertainly over him. Willows. Garrett Willows. Wasn't that what Magnolia had said? Was he Bethany's husband, then? The idea seriously rankled.

Chandler shoved up to his feet and pointed a finger. "*He* attacked *me!*"

"Chandler?"

Hearing Bethany's voice, Chandler whirled. She stood beneath the porte cochere with Hypatia and Odelia, her cornflower blue eyes wide.

"Why are you fighting with my brother?"

Brother. He glanced at Garrett Willows. His aunts' gardener was Bethany's *brother?*

She looked as stunned as Chandler felt—and stunning. In dark brown leggings and a long pink top with tiny puffed sleeves, her dark hair a silken fall to her shoulders, she looked wholesome and healthy and radiant. And pregnant, he reminded himself. And the *sister* of Garrett Willows, *not* the wife.

Chandler folded his arms and glared at his opponent. It wouldn't do to smile at such a moment. It wouldn't do at all.

Only a few moments earlier, in company with Hypatia and Odelia, Bethany had been on her way to the sunroom for breakfast. Then a grim-lipped Magnolia had emerged from the kitchen with a broom in hand, exclaiming that she had seen "them" fighting when she'd gone out to water the pot plants on the stoop. She'd stomped off toward the side door; Hypatia and Odelia had promptly followed, leaving a curious Bethany to bring up the rear. Bursting from the house, she'd seen two men rolling around on the ground and hitting each other. Magnolia had surged forward and smacked them both with her broom. When they'd fallen apart, Bethany had been shocked to see that one of them was her brother! And the other…Chandler! Chandler *Chatam?*

She shook her head. "I—I don't understand."

Her brother cast her a hooded glance and started to beat the dust from his jeans and bright blue T-shirt.

"Well, that makes two of us," Chandler said, glaring at Garrett. "What possessed you to come after me like that?"

Garrett ducked his head, muttering sullenly, "I saw you hiding in your truck around the corner of the building, and—"

"I wasn't hiding!" Chandler interrupted. "I was sleeping. I got back late and didn't want to wake anyone. I parked back there because I knew my aunts wouldn't want the horse trailer sitting where it could be seen from the street."

"Well, how was I supposed to know that?" Garrett snapped. To Bethany's shock, Garrett turned on her, demanding, "How on earth did you get involved with a Chatam, anyway?"

Before Bethany could answer, Hypatia stepped up and asked, "Do you two know each other?"

"No!" Bethany exclaimed.

At the same time, Chandler said, "Yes."

Odelia giggled and clapped a lace hanky between her hands, looking from one of her sisters to the other. "Didn't I tell you?"

Bethany had no idea what she was talking about, but it was difficult to take her seriously when she wore vivid yellow-and-white awning stripes, culminating with earrings fashioned to resemble stylized suns. They were almost as large as the visible ball in the sky overhead.

Hypatia made an exasperated sound and looked from Bethany to Chandler. "It can't be both."

"He told me his name was Chandler," Bethany blurted defensively.

"And it is," he drawled. "Hubner Chandler Chatam the third."

"You never said Chatam!" Bethany insisted.

"Oh, my word," Magnolia muttered.

Chandler sighed. "Look, it's just one of those crazy coincidences. I picked her up alongside the road about halfway between here and Houston."

"You were hitchhiking?" Garrett roared at her.

"No! I was trying to buy a bus ticket in a diner."

"But he said he picked you up alongside the road."

"The *diner* was alongside the road," Chandler stated pointedly.

"I don't care how you met him!" Garrett bawled. "What matters is that he's the father of your baby!"

There were audible gasps. Bethany gulped. Oh, how had this all gotten so muddled?

Chandler glared at her. "Did you tell him that *I* was the father?"

"No! I just didn't say that you *aren't* the father."

He parked his hands at his waist. "Come again?"

She opened her mouth to explain, heat burning her cheeks, when a pain seized her, so unexpected that she doubled over. "Ow!"

Both men rushed forward. Four strong arms surrounded her.

"Sis!"

"Bethany!"

"Ohhh," she moaned. "I-It's just a c-cramp."

"Bring her inside," Hypatia instructed smartly.

Chandler stepped back so Garrett could sweep her up in his arms, but the cramp was already waning.

"It's all right," she gasped. "Really. I—I can walk."

Everyone ignored her, moving en masse toward the house. Chandler leaped ahead and held open the bright yellow door as the sisters swept through. On their heels, Garrett carried Bethany inside, striding swiftly down the shadowy back hall to the family room.

"Honestly," she protested. "You don't have to carry me."

"It's either him or me," Chandler growled.

Bethany glanced over Garrett's shoulder at him. Despite needing a shave and looking somewhat haggard, the man was handsome enough to make a girl's heart go pitter-patter. And a Chatam! Her mind whirling, she quickly looked away.

Garrett carried her to a plush love seat, which matched the oversize sofa in the center of the room, where he at last set her on her feet. Stalling for time, Bethany tugged at the hem of her tunic and adjusted the tiny, puffed sleeves before smoothing her hands across the thighs of her brown knit leggings before sitting down. The Chatam sisters primly seated themselves on the full-length sofa. The men stood opposite each other, arms folded.

"Now, then," Hypatia said calmly, "I think we all need to know just who the father of this child is."

Bethany bowed her head. Could the situation be any more mortifying? It wasn't just embarrassing, though; it was dangerous, and she had to think of her child first.

She gulped and mumbled, "I can't tell you."

"But it's not Chandler?" Hypatia pressed.

Bethany shook her head, gaze averted.

"Satisfied?" Chandler asked, glaring at Garrett.

"How was I to know?" Garrett demanded. "She shows up, pregnant and unmarried, with you." Bethany flinched, hearing it stated so baldly. "All she'll say is that the father doesn't want the kid," he barreled on, "and you take off without even bothering to meet me!"

"I had important business! And why would I bother meeting you? I didn't know you were her brother. All I knew was that you're the gardener here, and I don't report to the gardener!"

"Stop it!" Bethany cried, shocking even herself. "Just stop snarling at each other. Neither of you has any reason."

"No reason?" Chandler demanded. "He hit me!"

"You hit me back," Garrett grumbled, rubbing his ribs.

Bethany sighed. Her eyes filled, and she bit her lip, but

then she managed to say softly, "I don't want to talk about who the father of this baby is anymore."

Garrett shifted. "But—"

"You heard her," Chandler snapped. Bethany glanced up, straight into his warm brown gaze. "It's her business," he muttered, glancing away.

"Of course." Hypatia said, as if that settled the matter.

"You're right," Magnolia agreed at the same time. Garrett looked like he might explode for a moment, but then he gave his head a sharp nod.

"Well, that's that, then," Odelia announced with some satisfaction. "And now we're all friends."

Bethany choked back a startled laugh. Then a weight seemed to descend on her shoulders. These were good people, every one of them. Her brother had offered her support when she needed it most. The Chatam triplets had taken her into their home without a moment's hesitation. Chandler had offered her a ride when she was nothing more than a desperate stranger stranded beside the road. Good people, indeed, and good people deserved the truth.

But she couldn't give it to them. Not now. Not ever.

She gulped and closed her eyes, remembering the look on Jay's face when he'd learned that she was pregnant. He didn't want this child, but he would take it from her if she ever told anyone what he'd done. With her family history and his resources, that would be too difficult.

Silence reigned for a long moment, then Garrett turned to face Chandler and squared his shoulders. They were both beginning to show a few scrapes and bruises but nothing that wouldn't be gone by morning.

"I apologize," he said. "I have a history of overreacting where the women in my family are concerned."

Chandler shrugged, his gaze skimming over Bethany. "No real harm done, I guess."

Garrett nodded curtly and moved to stand at her side, saying, "You have to admit that it's a lulu of a coincidence, my sister stumbling into your path."

"No kidding," Bethany murmured. Even Chandler lifted his eyebrows and nodded in agreement. Not so the triplets.

Hypatia shared an amused look with her sisters and calmly said, "Oh, my dears, do you not realize that for God's children, there are no coincidences? Only plans."

Chapter Four

Straightening, Chandler felt an eerie feeling skitter up his spine.

No coincidences for God's children.

Chandler knew that God had plans for the lives of believers, but he'd never before thought of it in quite that way. He suddenly remembered his father speaking from the pulpit.

"God allows nothing into our lives without a reason."

As a teenager, Chandler hadn't paid much attention, already at odds with his dad over his friendship with Kreger. Both he and Kreger had been horse-mad and dreaming of careers in rodeo. Pat's grandfather had encouraged their interest, but Hub believed that sports were frivolous, mere hobbies, certainly not occupations fit for Chandler men. Only lately, since Chandler's sister, Kaylie, had married a pro hockey goalie, had Hub rethought his prejudice somewhat.

Now, suddenly, Chandler heard his father's long-ago words with a different ear and applied that new interpretation to his meeting Bethany.

If Kreger had flown in to compete as they'd planned, he'd have been riding with Chandler back to Buffalo Creek. They wouldn't have left for home early that morning because Pat never hauled himself out of bed before he had to, which meant they'd have stopped for dinner long before they'd have reached that little diner. The only reasonable conclusion was that Chandler would have missed Bethany completely if things had gone as *he* had planned. No telling where she'd have wound up then.

A fresh chill ran up his spine, and he found himself wholly identifying with Garrett's impulses. If Bethany was his sister... But she was not his sister. She was, instead, a very attractive, *single* woman.

A single *expectant mother*, he reminded himself.

No, Chandler didn't blame Garrett for wanting to pound someone.

His ears perked up when Magnolia asked Bethany if she still intended to look for a job. Putting aside his thoughts, he listened to Bethany reply, "As quickly as possible."

"Sis, do you really think anyone is going to hire a woman as pregnant as you are?" Garrett asked, looking down at her.

Bethany sighed but otherwise did not answer.

"It is a problem," Hypatia agreed gently.

"I can't just live off your generosity and my brother's until the baby comes," Bethany pointed out.

Chandler surprised himself by speaking the instant the thought entered his mind.

"Dad might be willing to hire her."

Five pairs of eyes turned to him. Well, it only seemed logical. In fact, he was surprised that his aunts hadn't thought of it themselves. He cleared his throat and said, "Dad is about to open the new Single Parents Ministry to the public, isn't he?"

Hypatia brightened. "That's right. He's been talking about hiring a receptionist."

"That would be perfect," Bethany said, sitting forward. "What do they do there?"

"Offer parenting classes, support groups, Bible studies," Hypatia said. "They've also put together a panel of advisers, attorneys, mental health professionals, charities, anyone who can help lighten the load of a single parent."

"It sounds wonderful!" Bethany gushed.

"It's part-time, so the pay wouldn't be much," Magnolia warned.

"Still, it's something," Bethany pointed out.

"And of course you'll stay here until after the baby comes and you're on your feet again," Odelia put in.

For the second time that morning, Chandler watched Bethany's eyes fill with tears. She reached a hand up to her brother, who pressed her fingers with his, smiling.

"Looks like God brought both of us to the right place," she noted in a shaky voice.

"You'd think I'd learn to let Him handle things, wouldn't you?" Garrett said with a guilty glance in Chandler's direction.

Bethany chuckled and wiped tears from her cheeks. "That's something I guess we both have to work on."

Watching those slender fingertips swipe at the moisture on her ivory cheeks, Chandler felt a lump rise in his own throat and shifted uncomfortably. He realized suddenly that it was past time for him to be about his own business, even if he was tired due to lack of sleep. That, he told himself stoutly, was what was behind this sudden emotionalism, surely.

"How soon do you think I can speak to your father about the job?" Bethany asked him.

Chandler opened his mouth, but Hypatia spoke first.

"Chandler, dear," she said, "might you take Bethany to meet your father Monday?"

"Me?"

"That will give us time to speak to Hubner about it before-hand," Hypatia said to Bethany.

"Grease the skids, in other words," Garrett said wryly.

Magnolia laughed and quipped, "I'll get out the oil can."

Meanwhile, Hypatia answered Chandler. "Of course *you,* dear. You're the perfect person to do it."

Chandler flung a hand at Garrett. "Why not him?"

"On the back of my motorcycle?" Garrett retorted, shaking his head. "Not in her condition."

"And Chester is busy," Odelia informed him helpfully, "especially Monday. It's Hilda's shopping day, you know."

The aunties themselves did not drive. Chandler thought of his appointment with his cousin, the attorney, on Monday and a hundred and one other things he needed to get done as quickly as possible, but he knew that he had to do this. Talking to his dad about a job had been his idea in the first place, and Bethany was not getting on the back of that motorcycle if he could prevent it.

"Yeah, okay, fine," he said with less grace than he might have. "Now if that's settled, I'm going to move most of my stuff into the attic."

"You're moving in here?" Garrett asked, his brows drawing together.

Chandler rose. "Yeah. You have a problem with that?"

"No, of course not. Just surprised."

"That makes two of us," Chandler muttered. He purposefully did not look at Bethany, but turned to dispense kisses to the papery cool cheeks of his aunties, thanking them for their hospitality.

"Don't worry," Hypatia said, beaming a smile, "It's a very big house."

"The east suite should suit," Magnolia began, but Chandler waved that away.

"Naw, I'll just take one of the big bedrooms."

"In that case," Odelia chirped, "perhaps the room behind

the attic stairs? It has a window and is convenient to the attic."

Chandler shrugged. "Fine with me."

"Perfect!" Odelia exclaimed, clapping her hands. "That's right next to the master suite where Bethany and Garrett are staying."

Chandler raised his eyebrows. Evidently, the aunties were going all out in their support of the Willows siblings. Well, it was no skin off his nose, especially when they were willing to house him, too. But not for long, God willing, not for long. In fact, with single, pretty Bethany in residence, the sooner he got his business in order and moved out of Chatam House, the better.

It was all he could do to keep from looking at her one more time before he stepped out into the corridor and strode toward the library.

"I'll give you a hand."

Chandler glanced over his shoulder at Bethany's brother.

"That's not necessary."

"No, I insist."

O-o-o-kay, Chandler thought, wondering if Garrett was about to warn him away from his sister. Not that Garrett had anything to worry about. The very last thing Chandler needed in his life right now was a woman, especially a pregnant woman.

"Your breakfast will be waiting in the kitchen when you're done," Hypatia called.

Chandler brightened, thinking of Hilda's excellent cooking. "A ray of light in an otherwise dim world," he retorted drolly.

"If that means Hilda's cooking is the best, I couldn't agree more," Garrett said, lengthening his stride to bring himself even with Chandler.

Chandler shook his head. "First you try to beat me down and then you jump over into the amen corner."

"For the record," Garrett retorted, keeping pace with Chandler, "I *did* beat you down."

"In your dreams, brother."

"I'm not *your* brother."

Chandler snorted. "You could be. Neither of them can throw a decent punch, either."

"Now you've gone from dreaming to sheer insanity," Garrett said drily, and for some reason they were both suddenly grinning. "You handle yourself pretty well, too, though."

"Thanks," Chandler drawled.

"So where'd you learn to fight like that, anyway?"

"I rodeo for a living," Chandler replied. "There's always some drunk cowboy wanting to take you down a peg." The truth was that he hadn't been in a real fight in ages, but early on the occasional fracas into which Kreger had dragged him had almost seemed, well, fun. "How about you?"

Garrett paused just outside the library door and met Chandler's gaze. "Prison," he answered grimly.

Chandler rocked back. "Yeah? How come?"

Garrett sighed. "Like I said, I've been known to be a little overprotective of the women in my family."

"Do my aunts know about this?"

"Absolutely. I just thought you should know, too."

Chandler folded his arms. "Suppose you clue me in, then."

"Okay, but let's do it while we're working. Breakfast is calling me."

Chandler could find no argument against that, and later, having heard the full story, he could find no quarrel with Garrett's presence in the household, either. In fact, in his opinion, though he didn't know Bethany's story, the Willows siblings appeared to have gotten a pretty raw deal in life so far.

"God allows nothing into our lives without a reason," whispered his father's voice then, and right behind it came Hypatia's. *"Do you not realize that for God's children, there are no coincidences? Only plans."*

Chandler supposed that one's actions and decisions played into what God allowed and planned for a believer. Everyone had free will, after all. Still, a loving, omniscient God could be trusted to have reasons and plans, which meant that whatever was going on with him now, God had allowed for His own purposes. Chandler believed that those purposes would ultimately work for his benefit, for God did not curse his own children; He blessed them. Chandler knew that his life had been greatly blessed, especially compared to the lives of Garrett and Bethany Willows.

As he sat down with Garrett at the battered table in the warm, spacious kitchen to eat Hilda's fluffy scrambled eggs and crisp bacon, his situation suddenly looked a lot better than it had only last night, and Chandler determined to move forward prayerfully. With that in mind, he took the time to give silent thanks.

For this food and all the blessings in my life, Lord, I give You thanks, especially for the fresh perspective. Guess I needed that, and whatever else You will also surely provide. Seems like I forgot that. I'm sorry. Won't happen again. But if You could speed things up so I can get out on my own again, I'd sure appreciate it. He chuckled. *And a little patience on my part wouldn't hurt, either.*

When he looked up, he found Garrett Willows watching him. Chandler smiled. "Trying to turn over a new leaf."

Garrett arched a dark eyebrow at that, muttering, "Lot of that going on here."

Chandler glanced around the homey, old-fashioned,

redbrick and stainless-steel kitchen. Where better to get a fresh start, he asked himself, than here at Chatam House?

Now if only he could find a new partner and win some money… That, too, he decided he would leave in God's hands. Surely, with a little prayer and patience, it would all work out. After all, for God's children, there were no coincidences, only plans. And God's plans, he finally realized, had to be far superior to his own.

They could hardly be worse!

Fitting his left boot into the stirrup, Chandler grasped the horn with his left hand and swung up into the saddle. He shook out his loop. Sensing that they were about to go to work, the big bay, named Red Rover, danced until Chandler reined him to a standstill.

A good night's rest had cleared Chandler's mind. He'd spent the previous day making phone calls and settling into his room. Immediately after an excellent dinner, he'd turned in, as much to escape Bethany's unsettling presence as to be well rested for today's activity. She was a complication he didn't need, and now she was there in the house with him. Sure, it was a big house. He just hoped it was big enough. He needed all of his concentration if he was going to make this work; his very future depended on it.

He'd been surprised and pleased yesterday to find that Drew Shaw, a saddle bronc rider and one the finest heelers that rodeo had ever known, was on the lookout for a new partner, his previous header having retired. Chandler had eagerly made this appointment and driven to Stephenville, some two hours east of Buffalo Creek, and this modest private arena on the edge of town. This, he mused, might be the most important Saturday morning of his entire career.

Feeling as nervous as the quivering horse, he backed the big bay into place. They had been practicing for nearly an hour now, but this would be for time. Drew and his mount, a beautiful chestnut sorrel, already waited in their box. Chandler looked at Drew, who sat poised with lasso in hand, and signaled the chute man.

An instant later, the yearling steer shot past. The penalty line broke from the steer's neck and the barrier rope dropped away. Chandler spurred the bay, who leaped into action, instantly matching stride with the steer. Operating on practice and instinct, Chandler felt the loop leave his hand, saw it drop around the steer's horns. Perhaps two seconds later, Drew threw down his own loop and closed it. Chandler turned his bay, and in a blink, the steer was immobilized.

"Time!" shouted Drew's wife, Cindy.

She stood on the second-from-the-bottom rung of the metal-rod arena fence, her belly protruding between rods, a stopwatch in one hand. Chandler had been secretly amused to arrive and find the statuesque blonde pregnant. Seemed like pregnant women were becoming the norm in his life. Maybe he should've brought Bethany along today. She might have enjoyed the outing.

Then again, maybe not. The last thing he needed just now was a distraction, and Bethany Willows was proving to be just that. He couldn't seem to stop thinking about her, wondering why God had placed her in his path that day.

Drew loosed the steer, coiled his rope and rode over to the fence to take a look at the stopwatch. He then turned and rode toward Chandler, who hung his coiled rope on the saddle horn. A smile split Drew's round, freckled face.

"Pretty good. Let's take three or four runs at it and get an average. What do you say?"

"Sure thing."

After another hour, they called a halt, walking their horses to cool them down. As Chandler took care of his bay, he ran over the morning's work in his mind. In all honesty, Drew's technique was technically perfect but not nearly as showy as Kreger's. Chandler missed that flamboyance and enthusiasm, but he was smart enough to know that Drew's businesslike approach could be the competitive edge that would put them on top as a team. Drew, in fact, was not the one whose skills were on trial here.

Lord, he prayed silently, as he strolled over to Drew's rig, *let me measure up.*

"So what do you think?" he asked. His heart was beating like a big brass drum.

Leaning against the fender of his pristine, late-model dualie, Drew removed his pale straw hat, revealing thin, light brown hair, and refit it to his head. His wife stood next to him, her arms folded. Just a few inches shorter than Drew, she wore a T-shirt that didn't quite cover the elastic inset in her jeans and big, white-framed sunshades, her streaky gold hair pulled back into a short ponytail.

"Looks like we might fit," Drew said.

"In the arena, anyway," Cindy put in.

Chandler said nothing to that, knowing that it had portent he didn't quite understand. Drew's pleasant expression never altered, but the pale hazel eyes that met Chandler's were blatantly measuring. "We're not party folk," he said. "We don't go to the bars and lay out at night."

"I don't, either," Chandler told him, "not as a habit."

"That's not what we heard," Cindy said bluntly.

Chandler felt his stomach drop. It was true that he'd waded through more than his fair share of dives, but only to haul Kreger out of one jamb or another. He wouldn't use Pat as an excuse, though. In all truth, he had *chosen* to become Pat Kreger's keeper, and now he was paying for it.

"I don't know what you've heard," he said, "but frankly I'll be happy if I never have to walk into another bar."

A long look passed between husband and wife before Drew

nodded at Chandler and said, "We'll pray on it and get back to you."

A relieved smile pushed up from Chandler's chest. "And I'll do the same. Can't make a mistake that way, can we?"

"Not if we're letting the Lord lead," Drew said with a grin. The two men shook hands, and Chandler took his leave.

"Okay, Lord," he said from behind the wheel of his truck as he headed back to Buffalo Creek, "it's all up to You now. If nothing else, You've shown me a better way of doing things, and I can see that I need to make some adjustments."

He'd start with regularly attending worship services, he decided. He often attended Cowboy Church when he was competing, but not every rodeo boasted a Cowboy Church pastor. On those weekends when he was home, he avoided church. More accurately, he avoided his father by staying home, but he knew that had to change, starting tomorrow.

The thought flitted through his mind that at some point he'd have to choke down his pride and admit to his dad that he was right about Kreger, but Chandler let that notion go on its way. He had enough to think about already. More than enough. If one of the things occupying his mind lately was pretty, dark-haired and pregnant, well, better her than his ongoing battle with his father. Wasn't like he had much choice about it, anyway. She was in his head whether he wanted her to be or not.

"Garrett? Bethany? Are you riding with us?"

Magnolia's voice came to Chandler through his bedroom door. Mechanically looping his tie and fashioning a knot, he wandered over and shouldered the door open. Magnolia stood in front of the sitting room of the master suite. Bethany appeared from inside, holding closed her faded cotton bath-robe at the throat. It would not close over her distended belly or the knit shorts and top that she wore beneath it. She smiled sleepily at Magnolia.

"Good morning. Garrett's already gone down."

"Bethany," Magnolia said, "you're not dressed. Aren't you going to church, dear?"

"Oh, I—I'm moving slowly this morning," she answered, shrugging.

Chandler spoke up before he even knew that he was going to. "She can ride with me. I'm not going to Sunday School, just worship."

"How thoughtful," Magnolia said, glancing toward him.

Leaning forward, Bethany followed Magnolia's line of sight. Letting his gaze roam over her, Chandler adjusted the knot of his tie and turned down the collar of the white shirt that he wore with a pair of dark blue jeans and his best ostrich quill boots. He realized that he was smiling and quickly looked away, but he couldn't help thinking that in addition to that pretty face and beautiful hair, Bethany had really nice legs. In fact, with her rumpled hair, bare feet and pregnant belly, she was the most feminine thing he'd ever seen.

Bethany shook her head at him. "Thank you, but I'm not feeling all that well this morning." She lifted a hand to her temple as if to say that her head hurt.

"Oh, I'm so sorry," Magnolia crooned. "Are you sure you'll be all right here alone? Would you like me to stay with you?"

"No, no," Bethany insisted. "I'll be fine. I'm going to get something to eat and rest a little more. You go on with the others, and I'll see you later."

"I'm not sure you should be alone," Magnolia said worriedly.

"I wouldn't let Garrett stay. I'm certainly not going to let you," Bethany told her firmly. "Besides, I have a phone here. I'll be fine."

"Well, if you're sure," Magnolia murmured.

"Go," Bethany ordered, smiling.

Magnolia nodded and hurried off, tossing a speaking look in Chandler's direction. He wasn't sure why or how Bethany Willows had suddenly become his responsibility, but God knew the woman needed someone to look out for her and since her brother wasn't around, he supposed he was elected. He ambled down the short hall and leaned a shoulder against the doorjamb of the sitting room door.

"You know that the staff have Sundays off, don't you?"

"Yes, Garrett told me."

"I was going to grab a bite to eat on my way to church. I can bring something back for you, if you like. Won't take long."

Bethany smiled. "Thanks but that's not necessary. I'll go down and rummage around the kitchen in a little while, toast an English muffin or something. Garrett says Hilda makes her own."

"She does," Chandler confirmed, straightening away from the door frame.

"Great! Well, I won't keep you." With that, Bethany backed into the room and closed the door.

Chandler stood for a moment, telling himself that she was an adult fully capable of making her own breakfast. On the other hand, if she was feeling unwell, it wouldn't hurt him to toast an English muffin. Aunt Mags would undoubtedly expect it of him. He headed down to the kitchen.

Listening to the sounds of Chandler's footsteps as he moved away, Bethany let out a sigh of relief. Then she pushed away from the door, turned and caught sight of herself in the mirror over the sitting room mantle. Groaning, she stared at her rumpled hair and pale face, recalling how handsome he'd looked in his Sunday best, his face cleanly shaven, blond hair neatly combed. She looked as if she'd passed a rough night, when in fact the opposite was true.

She'd slept soundly, but she'd awakened in a panic, knowing that if she went to church this morning, she was bound to run into someone who'd known her back in high school, someone who remembered her elopement, someone who would undoubtedly ask about her obviously absent husband. She just couldn't face that yet. It was simply too embarrassing, especially while she was carrying this belly around.

Walking over to the Victorian sofa, she plopped down, frowning. What did she say when, inevitably, someone asked about her husband? That she was unmarried, never married, divorced, perhaps? She didn't want to lie, but she didn't want the truth out there, either, for numerous reasons. She slumped back against the sofa cushion, telling herself that she couldn't hide forever. Sooner or later, she would have to face this dilemma.

She mulled the problem but had found no solution when someone tapped on her door again a few moments later. Wondering who that could be now, she got up to answer, only to find Chandler Chatam standing there, a china plate in one hand and a glass of orange juice in another.

He thrust the plate and juice at her, saying, "You can stick those in the dumbwaiter when you're through with them." As he sauntered off toward his own room, he nodded toward the tiny elevator set into the wall at the end of the hallway. It came out downstairs in the butler's pantry, as she had discovered on her first day here.

Bethany looked down at the plate in her hand. It contained an unpeeled banana, a toasted English muffin and generous dollops of butter and some sort of jam. For a moment, she couldn't do anything more than stand there and stare, but then her stomach rumbled hungrily. Suddenly she realized that he'd made her breakfast.

Galvanized, she called out, "Thank you!"

"You're welcome," came the disembodied reply.

Carefully closing the door, Bethany let her smile grow. Setting the glass of orange juice onto a small writing desk, she reached for the still-warm muffin and dipped it into the soft butter before biting into it. Slightly crunchy and dusted with cornmeal, it filled her mouth with delight. Chatam House, she decided, closing her eyes, was a very good place to be indeed. And these Chatams, they were something else. Chandler, for instance, was the very epitome of the man's man, yet, he was very thoughtful, kind, not to mention forgiving, helpful, handsome...

Oh, why couldn't she have met a man like him instead of Jay Carter? But the past could not be changed, and her future no longer had room for a man. Besides, what on earth would a man like Chandler Chatam want with a fool like her? And a child. Not exactly every man's dream package.

Jay's insidious voice whispered through her head.

"You think any other man is going to want you with your crazy background and a kid in tow?"

No, even if she could bring herself to trust again, she couldn't believe that a good man like Chandler Chatam would ever want her. Better that she should just concentrate on being a good mother to her child and forget about him. If only she could figure out how to do it.

Chapter Five

Shifting on the pew next to Odelia, Magnolia glanced up the broad central aisle of the sanctuary at Downtown Bible Church and noted that Garrett and Chandler were working their way through the throng together. One dark and one blond, they were the perfect foil for the coloring and good looks of the other. Magnolia knew that once Hubner laid eyes on Chandler, the current discussion would be at an end, and the sisters had not yet accomplished their purpose, which was to promote Bethany as a candidate for the job of receptionist at the Single Parents Ministry.

Looking back to her older brother, who stood in the aisle next to Hypatia, Magnolia tamped down her impatience. Hubner had been a wonderful pastor, and she was pleased that he'd taken on the administration of the Single Parents Ministry. Not too long ago, the Chatam sisters had feared that Hub had essentially checked out of his life. After being widowed for a second time, he had suffered a heart attack. His daughter, Kaylie, a nurse, had then moved in with him and nurtured him back to health, but no one had seemed able to coax him back into his life and ministry. Thankfully, God had accomplished that through Kaylie's marriage to Stephen Gallow, and no one was happier about it than Magnolia, but her brother could be unreasonable where his youngest son was concerned.

"So do you or do you not need a receptionist?" she demanded, ignoring the look of exasperation that Hypatia dropped on her.

"I will," Hubner hedged.

"The question," Hypatia said, "is not will you need a receptionist, but *when* will you need a receptionist."

Hubner shrugged and hitched his dress slacks up around his middle. It wasn't so much that Hub had a pot belly as that his already slender frame had more or less shrunk around it, making that a prominent feature, and his rigid, somewhat backward-leaning posture, an effect of his bifocal glasses, called attention to it.

"I suppose I'll have to start looking for someone soon," he said, lifting his cleft chin.

"Excellent," Magnolia replied. "We'll be sending over someone special for you to interview tomorrow."

Hubner shoved his glasses back up onto his nose and sighed. "This isn't one of your causes, is it, one of your lost sheep?"

"Not at all!" Odelia exclaimed. "Why, she's practically a member of the family. And who knows, if she and Chan—"

Magnolia elbowed her. Hypatia hastily spoke over the resulting yelp. "She's the sister of Garrett Willows, our gardener, and she's, er..."

"Going to have a baby!" Odelia whispered happily, loud enough to be heard yards away. She glared at Magnolia as if daring her to use the elbow again.

As if that would do any good. Magnolia rolled her eyes in exasperation.

Chandler and Garrett arrived just then, and Hypatia

rushed to head off any awkwardness between father and son. "Hubner, you remember our gardener, Garrett Willows."

"Sir," Garrett said, shaking hands with the older man. "Nice to see you again."

Hubner smiled and nodded. His gaze then shifted to Chandler, whom he greeted with raised eyebrows. "Well, well," he said. "Will wonders never cease? It's Sunday, and my son is actually in church."

Magnolia sighed at the same time as Chandler. Why was it, she wondered, that Hubner could extend the hand of non-judgmental fellowship to any stranger on the street and yet greet his own son with such barbed criticism? She supposed that it had something to do with a father's expectations of his son and the son's need to go his own way.

"Hello, Dad," Chandler said sarcastically. "Nice to see you, too."

Magnolia verbally jumped between them before things could get out of control. "We're so pleased to have Chandler living at Chatam House now."

Hubner blinked. "Living at Chatam House? With Patrick Kreger?"

"No, of course not with Kreger," Chandler snapped, "and it's only temporary."

Hypatia hastily changed the subject. "Have you heard from Kaylie and Stephen?"

Hub pursed his mouth and briefly bowed his head, but he surrendered to the change of subject. Smiling tightly, he replied, "She's anxious to get back here to oversee the construction of the new house. I think Stephen is less enthused about the house than about getting in condition for the hockey season."

"That's understandable," Magnolia said, "given what he's been through since his accident." That set Hub off on a long report on Stephen's current condition.

Stephen had accidentally driven his car through a garage wall and injured himself severely. Thanks to the influence of Dr. Brooks Leland, Stephen had wound up recuperating at Chatam House in an effort to avoid the press. There he had met Kaylie, who'd been hired to oversee his care. The two had quickly fallen in love and were now on an extended honeymoon. They had sold Stephen's Fort Worth house and were now building a beautiful new home on the east side of Buffalo Creek. When it was finished, Hub intended to move in with them, at Stephen's invitation. Magnolia and her sisters were grateful for that, as it meant that they did not have to worry about Hub being cared for as he aged. They themselves had cared for their widowed father until his passing, but Hub was only a few years older than them.

"All in all, he's doing very well," Hub said, winding up.

Thankfully, the service was starting by the time the subject had been exhausted, and Hypatia hurried everyone into seats. Chandler sank down between Magnolia and Garrett. She caught a look of sympathy on Garrett's face and told herself wryly that her nephew may have made a friend between blows. Stranger things, as she well knew, had happened. Why, they had happened to another of her nephews, Reeves Leland, who had met and married an old childhood nemesis, Anna Miranda Burdett, at Chatam House just this past winter.

Suddenly Magnolia wondered if Odelia might not be right after all. She thought of the way Chandler had stood up for Bethany when she'd refused to name her baby's father and how he'd proposed that his father should employ her. Magnolia remembered, too, how studiously he'd tried not to glance in Bethany's direction at dinner last night, then how he'd offered her a ride to church this morning. Could it be that Odelia was right and romance was blossoming at Chatam House again?

Stranger things indeed.

Magnolia smiled, wondering if it would be wrong to give God just a little bit of a helping hand.

Stepping up onto the low, concrete stoop of the 1960s-era, ranch-style, brick house that was the headquarters for the Single Parents Ministry, Chandler reached out to pull open the heavy, commercial-type glass door and held it wide for Bethany to pass through. She was looking as businesslike as it was possible for a woman in her condition. Her short-sleeved navy blue dress featured an empire waistline with a skinny yellow belt that perfectly matched the narrow band holding back her dark hair and the soft, flat shoes on her slender feet. Whatever had kept her out of church the day before seemed to have passed, but she betrayed a certain nervousness when she paused on the threshold and pulled in a deep breath.

Chuckling, Chandler said, "I know just how you feel."

"Do you?"

"I'm looking for a new partner, and I had a tryout of sorts just last Saturday. I haven't been that nervous since I passed a note to Mary Ann Catcher in third grade."

"Check one if you like me. Check two if you don't," Bethany teased, paraphrasing an old country song.

Chandler grinned. "Something like that."

"And of course she checked number one."

"Actually, she stuck out her tongue and threw a pencil at me. Good pencil. I used it for a couple weeks."

They both laughed as the door swung closed behind them. The laughter took the edge off the dread that he felt at facing his father. It wasn't enough that he should give Bethany a ride over here this morning. Oh, no, Magnolia had privately insisted that he personally introduce her to Hubner, as if that would endear her to the old man. Still, Chandler would do his best.

Standing in the tiny entry hall of the converted house,

Chandler saw that straight ahead was what had obviously been the dining room, now fitted out with an old desk, a new computer and several thinly padded chairs to make a reception area. The living room, now a classroom, was on the right, with the kitchen tucked into the far corner next to the dining/reception space. Chandler imagined that the two or three rooms that opened off the hall to the left would be used for offices or storage.

His father came out of that hall, a smile on his face. "We're not officially open for another week," he was saying, "but if I can help you, I'll—" He stopped dead in his tracks, his jaw dropping.

Chandler hadn't expected quite that reaction. His father couldn't be *that* surprised to see him again so soon, and the aunts had surely mentioned Bethany to him the day before at church. Lifting a hand to the small of Bethany's back, he urged her forward, saying, "Dad, this is Bethany. She's looking for a job. The aunties thought I should introduce you to her myself."

Hub's face turned six shades of red. Confused by this reaction, Chandler shook his head, even as Hub bawled, "Chandler Chatam! Please tell me that you've married this girl!"

"Married!" Chandler echoed, knowing instantly what his father was thinking. So did Bethany.

"Not again," she moaned, casting Chandler an apologetic look. In high dudgeon, Hubner didn't even seem to notice.

"Odelia all but spilled it yesterday! Almost a member of the family! But I never dreamed that my own son would…" He shook a hand at Bethany, palm out, demanding of Chandler, "How could you?"

"But he didn't—" Bethany began.

Chandler grasped her wrist, squeezing hard enough to shut off the flow of her words. "No! Just forget it," he barked at her, glaring at Hub. "My father always knows best where I'm concerned. He knows all my thoughts, words and deeds. And each and every one is a disappointment to him. I've never done a right thing in my life so far as he's concerned! Don't even waste your breath. He's seen us together. He already knows everything he needs to know."

Bethany turned to him, lifting her hands to his chest, either to comfort or to calm him. "I'm sorry, Chandler," she whispered.

He shook his head. This was not her fault. "No, *I'm* sorry. I should have known better than to bring you to my father. Let's just go. You shouldn't be working, anyway." Hub always thought the worst of his youngest son, but this just plain hurt.

"Oh, no," she said. Pivoting on her heels, she fixed his father with a hard stare. "You go on to your appointment," she told Chandler firmly. "I'll be right here waiting when you get back."

"Bethany, this is not a good idea," Chandler argued. "He won't believe you."

"I'll be here when you get back," she stated again, meeting his gaze.

Those bright, cornflower blue eyes left him no option. Glumly, Chandler nodded. Shooting his father a bitter glance, he spun and shoved through the door. Once outside, he hesitated, breathing heavily. The impulse to stride back inside and sweep Bethany out of there was strong, but she had told him to go, and he had no right to overrule her.

Besides, Ash was waiting, and Chandler needed legal advice. Over the years, he'd poured more than fifty thousand dollars into the ranch that Kreger had just sold out from under him, and he needed to know if he had any legal redress, any hope of recouping some portion of his investment. Even now, he'd hate to have to sue his former friend, but perhaps he could levy a lien against the ranch.

And to think that he'd felt guilty about not telling his father about Kreger's lies! He'd certainly be keeping that to himself now.

Heavy of heart, Chandler went to his truck and slid inside. He glanced at the door to the house, now the offices of Single Parent Ministries, as proclaimed by the sign in the yard, and inserted the key into the ignition. Pausing, he beat down the need to go back inside and drag Bethany out of there. Finally, he started up the truck and reluctantly drove away.

The elderly man standing before her shifted his weight, his bushy eyebrows drawn together over the tops of his wire-rimmed glasses in a frown. All the Chatams, Bethany noted, seemed to have cleft chins. She brought her hands to her waist—or, rather, to where her waist had once been—and frowned right back at him.

"You are wrong about your son."

Dull red crept up Hub Chatam's throat from the open neck of his shirt collar, and he stuck out his chin. "My sister said yesterday that you were practically a member of the family. Then today he shows up here with you in that condition. What should I think?"

Bethany rolled her eyes. "My brother, Garrett, is the gardener at Chatam House. Your sisters treat him like he's a member of the family. I suppose that's what she meant. All I know is that they've been more than kind to me. They gave me a home when I had nowhere else to turn." She smoothed her hands over her belly as her muscles began to tighten.

"So you and Chandler both are living at Chatam House," Hubner said. "Well, that explains a good deal."

"Separately," Bethany pointed out. "We're not together. We moved in separately."

Hub scoffed at that. "I wouldn't expect anything else. But

if you and Chandler aren't together, why did he leave the ranch?"

She could only shake his head. "I don't know. That's his business."

"I see."

She doubted that, but she didn't feel like arguing just then. Her stomach muscles clenched painfully. "Do you mind if I sit down?" she asked, trying to relax. "I feel like I'm carrying around an anvil in here."

"Of course, of course." He swept a hand toward the desk. "This way." He waited for her to walk over and sit down, then pulled a chair close and sat facing her. "I must say…Bethany, is it?" She nodded. "I must say, Bethany, it's rather unusual for a woman in your condition to be out looking for a job."

"I don't see why. A woman in my condition has to live just like everyone else. I was working as a clerk in a convenience store until a couple weeks ago, but it's too hard now for me to stand on my feet all day."

"Ah. Well, the standing would be at a minimum here." He folded his hands and regarded her thoughtfully for some time before quietly saying, "I'm sorry for what Chandler has done—"

"Chandler has been very good to me," she interrupted sharply. "We first met beside the road *a few days ago,* and he brought me to my brother at Chatam House."

"And my sisters believed that tale?" Hubner exclaimed.

Meaning that he obviously did not! Exasperated, she started to get to her feet. "I see that Chandler was right. I'll just wait outside for him to return."

"I didn't say I wouldn't hire you," Hubner quickly told her, lifting a hand.

She sat back once more, surprised. "I can have the job? But why, if you don't believe me?"

"I can't imagine anyone else would hire you in this

condition, so, yes, you can have the job. It seems the best thing to do."

Bethany wasn't about to talk her way out of a paycheck by arguing further. Surely, in time, he would see that he was mistaken about her and his son.

"Thank you," she said.

"You're welcome, but there is a process to go through."

"Fine. No problem."

He rose then to go into his office for an application.

Bethany wondered what had occurred between father and son to foster such distrust on Hubner Chatam's part, but it was really none of her business. Besides, she needed this job, if only to pay her doctor bills. She knew that she had to have her cramps checked out, which meant that soon she had to find a doctor here in Buffalo Creek, and doctors expected payment.

Pastor Hub, as he told her to call him, went over a folder that outlined the ministry's objectives before leaving her to fill out the application. Bethany made short work of the form and eagerly scanned the list of programs and classes soon to be available.

"Oh, this is wonderful," she said when Hubner returned, "but you're open for business only three days a week?"

"Yes, that's right. Tuesday, Wednesday and Thursday. We have an emergency number that is answered through the church, and I don't mind telling you that I've been working much more than three days a week getting this off the ground. I hope to be able to cut back to that soon, and then eventually to hand off my duties to a younger person. I think perhaps I'll continue to teach some of the classes, though."

Part-time work was better than no work, Bethany mused. After the baby came, she could look for something better paying. Until then, this would have to do. They agreed that she would start first thing the next morning, primarily to field calls from people wanting information. They discussed her other duties, which were minimal, and then Hub showed her around the place.

Their business concluded, they wandered back to the reception area to resume their seats.

"Would you be offended if I said that I would pray for you?" Hub asked after a moment.

"Not a bit." Especially, she thought, since God did not always seem to hear her own prayers.

"Good, because I sense that you have been deeply hurt."

She didn't deny it, but quickly qualified, "Not by Chandler."

"Then perhaps you will tell me who it is that has hurt you," Hubner urged.

She met his gaze, quipping, "You want the whole list? Or just the worst one?"

"Let's start with the worst one," he said gently.

Her answer didn't even require thought. "My stepfather." Jay's perfidy barely even registered when compared with what Doyle Benjamin had done. "He murdered my mother."

Hub reared back in surprise, but then his expression softened into sympathy. "Oh, I remember now. A great tragedy."

She nodded, and they discussed that time in hushed tones, including how Garrett had gotten caught up in the fallout.

"I didn't realize that about your brother," Hub said, "but I'm glad you told me."

Chandler pushed through the door at that moment. He glowered at his father in silence, then switched his gaze to Bethany. "Ready to go?"

"Yes." She slid to the edge of her seat and paused, hoping Hub would apologize for his earlier behavior, but instead he lifted his chin and looked away. Heart sinking, she rose to her feet.

Hub, too, stood. Never taking his eyes off Bethany, he said, "I'll expect to see you tomorrow morning promptly at eight o'clock."

"I'll see you then."

He patted her shoulder, saying, "Casual attire. We want a relaxed atmosphere. No need to drag out your Sunday best."

"That's good," she replied wryly, "because this dress is about the extent of it."

Hub chuckled, and she answered with a smile before turning toward Chandler. He nodded, a pleased gleam in his warm cinnamon eyes. Whatever his problem with his father, he wasn't bothered by the idea of her working with the man. Bethany allowed Chandler to sweep her back out into the July heat. The two men never spoke to one another, but she was too happy to worry about it just then. Only later, in the front seat of Chandler's pickup truck, did she stop to think about that and its implications.

"I'm sorry if I created problems between you and your dad," she told Chandler sincerely.

He lifted an eyebrow at that. "Hardly. My father and I have had problems since I was in high school." He shifted in his seat then, adding, "I had a particular friend that my father did not approve of."

"Ah. But that was a while ago," she pointed out.

"Not long enough," Chandler drawled. Sighing, he admitted, "The truth is, Dad was right about my friend. It just took me this long to find it out."

"He's not right about you, though," she said. Chandler shot her a surprised look. "I mean, he wasn't right about you today."

"Nope."

"So, what makes you think he's right about your friend?"

Chandler shrugged, and she thought for a moment that he would fob her off with some clever, muddled quip. But then he gripped the steering wheel with both hands and told her how his "friend" had betrayed him and how slim his chances were, according to his attorney, of ever receiving restitution.

"That's why you're looking for another partner," Bethany said.

"That's why."

"And all that money is just gone?"

He literally squirmed over that. "Yeah, according to my cousin, the attorney. I was too stupid to insist on drawing up a contract or having my name put on the deed, and Ash doubts a lawsuit would succeed because I was living there, working there and keeping my horses there while I was giving Pat money. Even though we had a verbal agreement that half of it would go toward a down payment on my share of the ranch, it would be his word against mine, or at the very best, an arbitrated settlement that I already know Kreger can't pay."

"I'm so sorry," she told him softly. "I know what it feels like to trust someone with your future and be betrayed."

Turning a grim face toward her, Chandler shook his head. "It's nothing time and prayer can't resolve. Lots of time and prayer."

She couldn't help grinning at that. "You sound just like your father now."

He couldn't have looked more stunned if she'd belted him, but then he laughed. "Don't say any such thing to him. It's liable to give him another heart attack."

She gasped at that. "He has a bad heart?"

"No. He had a heart attack due to a blockage in one of his veins, but his heart is still strong. My sister, Kaylie, explained it all to us. She's a nurse."

"I see."

Bethany thought about what he'd told her. They had more

in common than she could have imagined, and she wasn't so sure that what had been done to her was so much worse than what Chandler was dealing with. Betrayal was betrayal. But at least he still had one parent. How sad that they should be at such odds.

"So what are you going to do now?" she asked. "Any plans?"

Chandler nodded. "I've placed my horses with a friend, and I've already been to see another man about taking me on as his partner. As soon as I get some money in hand, I'll find a place of my own. Until then…thank God for my aunties and Chatam House."

"Amen!"

"It's humbling, though," he said, tossing a wry smile her way. "Starting all over when you thought you were on the right track to begin with."

"Humbling," she echoed, nodding.

"And a little scary," he added.

She rubbed her hand over her belly. "No kidding."

"But it's going to be okay," Chandler said, sounding as if he was trying to convince himself as much as her. "Right?"

She looked up to find him watching her, concern etching a line between his brows. It was the same expression that his father had worn earlier, but she doubted that he would care to know that, so she merely smiled and told him what he wanted to hear.

"Yes, we're all going to be fine."

Somehow. Eventually.

She hoped.

"See you soon," Chandler said, offering his hand to Drew Shaw.

"Sure thing, partner," Drew said, grasping Chandler's hand in a hearty shake.

Chandler had been pleased and hopeful when Drew had called Tuesday to suggest that he come to Stephenville a few more times to see how things went with the two of them. Anxious to devote as much time to fostering this partnership as possible, Chandler had toyed with the idea of finding someone else to get Bethany to and from work. With his father working feverishly to get the ministry offices ready to go public next week, his sister out of town and Chester busy with the aunties, however, Chandler didn't know of anyone on whom he could call to give Bethany a ride. Magnolia had suggested his brother Morgan, but Chandler had thought of Morgan's fast little sports car and nixed that idea. He'd just have to make it to Stephenville and back while she was working.

After meeting with Drew Wednesday, Chandler had decided to withdraw from the individual events that he had entered and concentrate on securing a partnership with Drew. That paid off Friday, when Drew and Cindy offered him partnership papers. He'd taken them to Asher, who'd found no fault with them, and had carried them back this bright Saturday morning, signed, sealed and now delivered.

"I'll get those entries in today," Cindy said as Chandler slid behind the wheel of his truck. "If there are any problems, I'll let you know."

They had agreed that she would be the manager in this newly formed partnership, but she would not take care of Chandler's individual entries. Chandler had acted informally as manager for both him and Kreger, and neither had worried overmuch about who paid what, which meant that Chandler had paid most of the entry fees for both of them. Drew, on the other hand, had already set up a special bank account to handle their fees and winnings and an agreement on payouts. Very businesslike. For his part, Chandler had written a check to cover his half of the first entry fee. Hopefully, the next one would come from their joint winnings.

As he drove toward Buffalo Creek, Chandler let his mind wander. Drew had suggested that they debut their team at a rodeo in Lawton, Oklahoma. The purse wasn't huge, but the stock provider was well-known and the location was about equidistant for both of them. Cindy had confirmed that slots were still available, so Chandler had agreed.

A forthright woman, Cindy made Chandler think that she might be uncomfortable to live with, unlike Bethany who was sweetly willing to get along and go along. He didn't dislike Cindy, and Drew certainly seemed happy with her; Chandler just didn't think that he would be comfortable married to her.

Bethany, on the other hand, had an entirely different effect on him. She made him want things, a home and family of his own, someone to share his thoughts, concerns and joys with, someone who looked at him the way Cindy looked at Drew. It was nonsense, of course.

Chandler was in no position to offer Bethany, or any woman, anything, especially not the monetary kind. His rapidly dwindling bank account testified to that. He was happy to do what he could, of course, like driving her to and from work, and he was glad that the aunts had stepped up to provide a home for her, but Bethany's brother would have to manage the rest.

Chandler wondered idly just how much money Garrett made. The aunties were generous, but they couldn't be paying him much above minimum wage. Then again, they also provided housing and food. Still, he couldn't be taking in much, and working only three days a week, Bethany wouldn't be in a position to add to their joint coffers.

On the other hand, Chandler himself had nothing at all coming in just now and quite a lot going out, which meant that he had nothing to offer a woman at this point in his life. If things were different, though...

He mentally shook his head. Better not to even go there. The last thing any woman, even a pregnant and unmarried one, needed was a broke cowboy who couldn't even put a roof over his own head, let alone hers and her child's. Besides, Bethany didn't have any interest in him. Best he go about his own business and leave Bethany to God.

He was so distracted by his thoughts that he found himself pulling to a stop in front of the mansion rather than going on around to the side of the house. He decided to leave the truck right there for now, eager to share his good news with his aunts. Smiling to himself, he climbed up onto the porch and let himself in the front door.

Bethany practically fell into his arms, gasping, "I need a doctor!"

Barefoot and wearing only shorts and a T-shirt, she hunched over and grasped her belly, telling Chandler without words that the need was urgent. Scared half out of his boots, he swept her up into his arms, shouting for his aunts.

"They're at a meeting," she groaned. The aunties supported numerous causes, which meant that they could be anywhere in town, and wherever they were, Chester and the town car were with them.

Chandler didn't bother to suggest that they fetch her brother or wait for him to be informed. Instead, he practically ran across the porch with her, leaving the door standing wide open, and dropped her onto the backseat of his truck before sprinting around to jump beneath the steering wheel once more. Lights flashing, he drove her to the emergency room at Buffalo Creek Memorial Hospital as rapidly as possible, while she wept and moaned in obvious pain.

Terrified for her and the child, he went to the only place he knew to go to at such times, straight to the throne of God.

Chapter Six

Chandler brought the truck to a stop at the curb in front of the emergency room door and hopped out. Bethany slid to the edge of the seat and let him gather her into his arms.

He carried her through the automatic doors into the crowded waiting area, calling out, "We need some help here!"

Immediately, the crowd parted, and Chandler rushed toward a cubicle that contained a registration desk.

"She's in pain," he said to the woman behind that desk. "It's too early."

Within moments Bethany was being whisked into the treatment area by a nurse pushing a wheelchair. Chandler fell into step with the chair. The nurse began shooting questions at them, questions only Bethany could answer. Chandler was horrified to hear that she had been feeling a regular "tightening" since rising from her bed that morning and that in the last hour the "cramps" had become increasingly painful.

The nurse delivered them to a curtained bed, but when Bethany made to rise, Chandler lifted her into his arms once more and placed her on the gurney. Another nurse swooped in to take her vitals, while the first promised that a doctor would be with her shortly. The new nurse took a hospital gown from a stack on a nearby counter and shook it out. Chandler immediately stepped outside the curtain. The clerk from the front desk was waiting for him with a clipboard and ink pen in hand.

"Name?"

He answered without thinking, "Chandler Chatam."

"*Her* name."

"Bethany—"

She interrupted him, asking for and jotting down an address before thrusting the clipboard at him. "Sign here. You can take care of the rest later."

His mind whirling, he took the pen and signed.

The other nurse shoved back the drape. He hurried back to Bethany's bedside and took her hand in his again. Tears rolled from her eyes and into the hair at her temples.

"I'm scared," she whispered in a trembling voice.

"Gonna be okay," he promised, silently adding, *Please, Lord. Please!*

Clasping his hand, she nodded, but her chin wobbled. He reached back and pulled a hard plastic chair close, so he could sit right next to the bed. Someone came in with a machine of some sort and peeled away the covers and gown to bare Bethany's stomach. Embarrassed, Chandler kept his gaze trained on Bethany's face as she maintained her crushing grip on his hand.

Finally, the doctor came in. Like the nurses, she was no one that Chandler knew, no one that his sister, the nurse, or his older brother Morgan's best friend, Dr. Brooks Leland, had ever introduced. Brisk and efficient, with a blond pony-tail and a square, unadorned face, she identified herself as Dr. Andersen as she moved a rectangular instrument over Bethany's belly.

"Well, he's not in position," she noted after several moments of staring at a computer screen.

"He?" Bethany said, sniffing. "It's a boy?"

The doctor shot her a look. "Oh, did I spoil the surprise?"

Bethany shook her head. "No. They couldn't tell before." She looked at Chandler, whispering in a tone of wonder, "It's a boy."

A boy. Chandler gulped, his chest suddenly feeling as tight as a big brass drum. Bethany was going to have a son. Chandler wondered what he would look like and what his name would be. He wondered if he would ever have a son, and he knew that if he were ever so blessed he would storm the gates of heaven for that child.

He could do no less for Bethany's child. If he didn't, who would?

The doctor said that she needed to examine Bethany, so he hurriedly stepped outside the curtain once again. The examination seemed to take forever, but Chandler used every moment of it to silently plead for Bethany and her son, just as he would have if that little boy had been his own. He wished suddenly that this baby was his, and for the first time he felt the kind of paralyzing fear that Bethany must be feeling. It was not just sadness and pity, not just a detached sense of possible disaster, but a bone-deep terror that something too precious for words was at stake, something that could never be replaced and would forever be missed if God did not extend His great mercy at that very moment.

Closing his eyes, Chandler begged for that little life and the woman who carried it.

"What does it mean that he's not in position?" Bethany nervously asked the doctor.

"Means he's not ready to be born," the doctor told her, having finished her examination. "You're not ready, either."

One of the nurses opened the curtains and allowed Chandler back in. He came immediately to Bethany's side.

"You mean she's not in labor?" he asked, obviously having overheard.

"Not in real labor," the doctor said.

"Thank God!"

The doctor went on to explain about Braxton-Hicks, which she described as a sort of practice labor. Bethany breathed out a sigh of relief even as the doctor mentioned that stress often exacerbated the cramps. She'd had plenty of that lately, but Bethany determined not to waste one more moment worrying over the past.

"I'm going to order some meds, then if everything's okay in a couple hours, she can go home," the doctor said to Chandler. "Just make sure that she sees her OB-GYN as soon as possible."

Chandler opened his mouth, but then he closed it again and nodded. Bethany bit her lip. Obviously, the doctor thought Chandler was the father of her child. Bethany knew that she ought to correct that mistake, but she was too embarrassed to do so. Besides, what difference did it make when they might never see any of these people again? Chandler didn't speak up, so she reasoned that she should follow suit.

The doctor exited, leaving the curtains open. Nurses and techs came and went. After a while, the medicine did its stuff, and Bethany could finally relax.

She discussed with Chandler whether to call her brother and his aunts, and together they decided not to at this point. Why panic everyone when there was no crisis? She felt a little foolish about that, but Chandler insisted otherwise.

"Don't even go there. How were you supposed to know it was false labor? Even if you had suspected, you'd have had to be sure."

That was true. "You don't know how terrified I've been.

Every time I'd get one of those cramps, I'd worry that something was wrong."

"This has been going on for some time, then?"

"A few weeks."

"Didn't you discuss it with your doctor back in Humble?"

She shook her head. "I thought they were just cramps, so I intended to bring it up at my next scheduled visit. Then everything blew up, and I hit the road."

"Blew up?" he echoed, and Bethany could have bitten off her own tongue. "What do you mean?"

"Chandler!"

Another nurse suddenly breezed in through the opening in the curtain. Young and attractive, she wore pink scrubs and a surprised expression.

"Oh, hey, Linda. How are you?" Even as she let out a relieved sigh, Bethany cringed inwardly. So much for never seeing these people again! He looked at Bethany and made the introductions. "Linda, this is Bethany. Bethany, this is Linda Shocklea, a friend of my sister's."

"Everything okay here?" Linda asked.

"Yeah, I think so," Chandler replied. He gave her a quick explanation.

"Ah," said Linda. "Glad it's nothing more serious." She beamed at Chandler, exclaiming, "I haven't seen you in forever! What do you hear from that sister of yours?"

"*Nada*. She and Stephen should be home from their honeymoon soon, though."

"I knew they were hung up on each other even before I heard about the engagement," the woman said, sweetly smug, "but no one said anything about you! I didn't even know you were married, let alone about to be a daddy."

Chandler looked at Bethany. And said nothing.

Linda chattered on for a few minutes before the doctor

strolled in to announce that Bethany could go. Chandler turned a tight smile on Linda as he smoothly rose to his feet.

"Looks like they're kicking us out of here," he said needlessly. "Good to see you."

"You, too." She smiled at Bethany. "Nice to meet you."

Bethany nodded as the other woman turned away.

The nurse arrived as the doctor left and handed some papers to Chandler. He glanced over them and muttered, "Be right back."

Knowing that, at the very least, she owed him an apology, Bethany verbally reached out. "Chandler."

He turned back, glanced at the nurse, nodded grimly and slipped away before Bethany could say another word. She told herself that it would serve no purpose to blurt the truth now, but deep in her heart, she knew that she hadn't spoken because she was ashamed—and because she so desperately wished that Chandler *was* the father of her son.

Chandler knew that he should have set the record straight from the very beginning, but it hadn't occurred to him until it was too late, and now the whole hospital was going to think that he was married! That, however, was surely better than having everyone assume that he was about to become an unwed dad, as his very own father did. Besides, he couldn't bring himself to embarrass Bethany by blurting the truth of her situation, what he knew about it, anyway, which was that she was pregnant and unmarried. All in all, Chandler told himself, it might be easier just to marry the girl and forget about trying to explain this mess.

He carried the papers that the nurse had given him to the checkout desk and waited impatiently while a distraught woman argued with the implacable clerk. As he waited, he fished his wallet from his hip pocket. He wasn't responsible for the charges, of course, but Bethany certainly could not pay, and someone had to. Besides, as insane as it was, he *wanted* to pay. Or maybe what he wanted was to be what he was pretending to be, her husband and the father of her child. Like that could happen.

When his turn came, he laid down his debit card. He couldn't afford a family, he told himself, but he could manage this; then, when he saw the actual fee, his stomach dropped. This, he knew, was just the tip of a financial iceberg big enough, no doubt, to sink a battleship, let alone a struggling rodeo cowboy. She needed someone with a steady paycheck and a settled lifestyle. That being the case, he couldn't help wondering why God had allowed him to get caught up in this situation. God surely had a purpose, though, just as the aunts asserted. Maybe this was it, this one act, that and getting her to safety at Chatam House.

Stuffing the receipt into his pocket, he strode back toward the treatment area. Just as he was about to turn away, he caught sight of his truck still parked at the curb in front of the emergency room door. A yellow slip of paper fluttered in the breeze, caught between the wiper blade and the windshield. Groaning, Chandler rushed outside and snatched it free, knowing that he was going to find a parking ticket.

Okay, God, he prayed silently, *You've got my attention now. Big-time. Just tell me what You want, and You've got it. I've been stupid, and I've been foolish. Worse, I've been deaf, but I'm listening now. Just tell me what to do.*

On the trip home, Bethany apologized and apologized. Chandler shook his head, muttering about circumstances and misunderstandings, but Bethany felt awful about the whole thing, so awful that she didn't even think about the emergency room bill.

Garrett and the sisters had come in to find Bethany gone

and were on the verge of calling 911 when she and Chandler arrived. After a rushed explanation, Bethany took a seat in one of the comfortable armchairs at the end of the room. No sooner had she relaxed than Garrett asked how she'd paid the bill.

Bethany slapped her palms to her cheeks and gasped. "I didn't! I—I guess they're going to bill me."

Chandler, who had been prowling around the front parlor like a big, restless cougar ever since they'd come in, finally struck a pose, leaning against the ornate plaster mantle with his arms folded. "I took care of it."

While Bethany gaped, Garrett faced Chandler. "Why would you do that?"

Chandler shrugged. "Someone had to."

Garrett looked at him thoughtfully. "Thanks, man. I'll pay you back."

Chandler pushed away from the fireplace and strode toward the doorway, one hand reaching into his shirt pocket. He paused in front of Garrett and proffered a crumpled sheet of yellow paper. "Take care of this and we'll call it even," he said gruffly, walking out of the room.

Garrett smoothed the slip of paper against one palm, studying it, and turned a surprised expression on his sister. "It's a parking ticket. Illegal parking in an emergency zone."

The sisters traded looks before turning their gazes on Bethany. Magnolia tilted her head, saying, "Chandler seems awfully troubled over a simple parking ticket. Is there something you haven't told us, dear?"

Bethany couldn't bring herself to confess that Chandler had been mistaken for the father of her child. Again. Then she remembered the best news of all.

"I'm going to have a little boy!"

The sisters erupted with expressions of delight. Talk turned to such things as names. Bethany looked at Garrett and knew they were both thinking the same thing.

"Our father's name was Matthew," she noted softly.

Garrett smiled. "I'm sure Dad would have liked to have his grandson named after him."

Teary-eyed, Bethany beamed. The baby moved, seeming to roll from one side of her abdomen to the other. Grinning, she smoothed her hands over her distended middle. "I think he likes it, too!"

"Halfway there," Magnolia said approvingly. "Now all you need is a middle name."

"First, I need an OB-GYN," Bethany said. "I have to find a local doctor right away, but I've already called everyone in the phone book, and no one can see me."

"Time to call Brooks," Magnolia stated flatly. Rising, she went for the phone.

Ten minutes later, Bethany was speaking with Brooks Leland, general practitioner and Chatam family friend. After hearing what the emergency room physician had said, Dr. Leland promised to arrange an appointment for her with a colleague who was an OB-GYN, saying that his office would get back to her within forty-eight hours.

"Well," Hypatia declared after Bethany had ended the call, "we have much to give thanks for." She fixed Bethany with a regal eye, adding, "I'm sure you'll want to attend worship tomorrow in praise for today's blessings."

Smiling weakly, Bethany nodded, knowing that no excuse would be sufficient to keep her at home tomorrow. Accepting her fate, she tried not to dwell on the uncomfortable prospect of attending services at Downtown Bible Church. Perhaps everyone she had known had moved on by now. Perhaps she wouldn't even be recognized. Besides, Hypatia was right. She had too much to be thankful for *not* to attend worship.

Still, Bethany quailed at the thought of encountering old

friends who would undoubtedly ask about her "husband." Some might even remember Jay attending her mother's funeral with her. She tried to convince herself that it would be okay to say that she was divorced, but she didn't know if she could get the words out of her mouth. Perhaps she could just say that she was no longer married and pretend not to hear any other questions. Faint hope, at best.

Chandler missed dinner that evening, which was just as well, and he was nowhere to be seen again on Sunday morning, either. Somewhat relieved, Bethany got ready for church, wearing the same navy-and-yellow outfit that she had worn to her job interview, and allowed herself to be bundled into the sisters' town car. She even meekly submitted to being included in their senior women's Bible class, deeming that safer than seeking out women of her own age. She balked only when she found herself herded ahead of Garrett through the great arched sanctuary and into the center of a long pew already occupied by none other than Chandler Chatam. Bethany could do nothing but drop down next to him, smiling weakly.

He nodded in greeting, but he could not seem to keep still during the service, as antsy as a puppy. Bethany tried to concentrate on the sermon but was too aware of him to do so. Deeply thankful when the service ended, she rose and pushed as close to Garrett as possible while she waited to exit the pew. The Chatam sisters were in no apparent hurry, however, and stood in the crowded, busy aisle, chatting with various individuals. One of them, a rather portly old gentleman with a bald head undisguised by a thin comb-over, a rakish bow tie and a brass-headed cane, had attached himself to Odelia and showed no sign of moving out of the way. Garrett finally managed to ease out into the aisle behind him. Bethany had a bit more difficulty.

The only way she could slip past the old fellow was to lean as far back as possible to get her belly out of the way. Unfortunately, at the last moment, she stepped on a hymnal that had fallen unnoticed to the floor. The book slipped, and with it went her foot. She'd have toppled backward over the pew if Chandler had not lunged forward and scooped her against him.

For a long moment, they stood there, staring into each other's eyes, until she became aware that the sisters were anxiously inquiring as to her well-being.

"I'm fine," she told them, pulling away to finally step out into the aisle. "No harm done."

Chandler edged past her and quickly cleared the way, sweeping his long arm in a broad arc. Bethany ducked her head and doggedly began to weave her way around one cluster of individuals after another to the double doors at the back of the sanctuary. The instant she passed through those massive doors, however, she found herself face-to-face with the dreaded past.

"Bethany!"

Cleo Ann Mathis had once been Bethany's best friend. As girls, they'd shared sleepovers, birthdays and childish dreams, but as Bethany's home life had deteriorated, so had their friendship. By high school, they'd been nothing more than nodding acquaintances. The intervening years had been good to Cleo Ann. A little heavier, she now wore her light brown hair short and spiky and bleached almost white, but the smile was quintessential Cleo Ann. Quaking inside, Bethany allowed herself to be embraced.

"Hello, Cleo Ann."

"I can't believe this! Just look at you. No one said a word."

Who would, Bethany asked herself, with her brother gone from town, too?

A number of other women had gathered around by now. They began shooting questions at Bethany.

Bethany tried to order the questions in her mind. "Uh, d-due date is mid-October. It's a boy, and yes, I've moved back here."

"Let us give you a shower, then," someone said. "We'd be glad to."

Before she could decide how to reply to that, Cleo Ann asked, "So how and when did you two meet?"

Bethany looked at her old friend helplessly. You two?

Suddenly, a hand gripped her arm and a familiar voice said, "Excuse us, ladies. Gotta run."

Bethany felt herself propelled forward. Cleo Ann and the others called farewells, to which Bethany replied with an apologetic wave. Hurrying to keep up with Chandler's long strides, she allowed him to guide her through the foyer, out the front doors, along the sidewalk and around the corner to his truck, which was parked parallel to the curb.

"First the whole hospital, now the whole church," he muttered.

She gasped, reality crashing down. "They think we're married!"

"Big surprise, right?" he said, handing her up into the passenger seat.

Moaning, Bethany dropped her head into her hands while he jogged around to the driver's side. "Oh, Chandler, I'm so sorry. I never meant for any of this to happen. I didn't even mean to sit next to you in church! Why didn't you say something this time?"

"You think I should've whistled everyone to attention and announced that I am not the father of your child? That would've gone over great." He started up the engine and pulled away from the curb.

"Why didn't you just walk away, then?" she asked, tears clogging her throat.

"So you could do what? Tell everyone that you're pregnant and unmarried?"

"That's better than them believing that we're married to each other!"

"Really? And who do you suppose they would think the father is, anyway? Especially after yesterday."

Bethany wept. This was even worse than her worst fears. "I don't mean to keep dragging you into this. Honestly, I don't."

Chandler sighed and pulled the truck over again to loop an arm loosely about her shoulders. "I know that, and I'm not mad, I'm just… I don't know what I am."

"You're too good, is what you are," Bethany managed, wiping her eyes. "You're just too good."

"All I am," he said, shaking his head ruefully, "is confused. I'm just trying to figure out what God is doing in my life. I just want to know what He wants of me."

"That makes two of us," she told him.

"Well," he said, "I expect we'll find out soon enough. Let's just hope it includes the whole town figuring out that they're wrong about us."

"No kidding," she muttered. They couldn't have been more wrong, in fact, no matter how much she might wish otherwise.

For some reason, he laughed. She didn't know why, but she smiled.

Nothing had changed. It was still the most awkward situation she could imagine, but for the moment, just being able to smile was enough.

Chapter Seven

Wondering whose luxury sedan stood parked in front of the house, Chandler hopped out of the truck and followed Bethany up the brick walkway and onto the stoop beneath the porte cochere. He had forgone practice with Drew today to take Bethany to her doctor's appointment, which had apparently gone well. It seemed that a lot of first-time mothers had Braxton-Hicks contractions.

"And very few of them actually deliver early," Bethany was saying.

"That's a relief," he replied absently, reaching around her to pull open the bright yellow door.

She went before him into the darkened back hall, lighting it up with her sleeveless lime-green knit dress. Her sleek, dark hair bounced in a jaunty ponytail at the crown of her head.

"Plus," she went on blithely, "they'll let me prepay the fee."

"Excellent." He wondered silently how long that would take.

They came to the central hall and made the turn that would take them to the foyer, but before they got that far, Magnolia appeared from the direction of the front parlor. He noticed her rigid posture and the grim line of her mouth, as well as a fearful hardness about her eyes. Even more worrisome, the loud, cheery tone with which she addressed them sounded patently false.

"Hello, dear ones! We've been waiting for you. You have a caller, Bethany dear, a Mr. Haddon." Chandler glanced at Bethany, who shook her head. Mags leaned closer and said, "He's an attorney."

Bethany's blue eyes widened. "An attorney? What does he want?"

"He wouldn't tell us," Magnolia hissed, "and I don't like it one bit."

Chandler could see the pulse leaping in the hollow of Bethany's throat and instinctively stepped closer to her. Gulping, she looked up into his eyes, and he saw at once that she was frightened, but she turned and stiffly followed Magnolia into the parlor. He went with her, determined not to let her out of his sight.

Defying habit, the aunties had parked their guest in the front section of the spacious room where three stiff, scroll-armed chairs, placed perpendicular to the front window, faced a hard-backed, carved oak settee. Perched on the settee was a tall, slender man in his forties with a beaked nose, freckles and an abundance of neatly trimmed, cinnamon-and-sugar hair. His paleness, coupled with the pale natural linen suit that he wore with a white shirt and beige tie, made his obsidian eyes seem reptilian. He had evidently refused tea, a fact that could not have endeared him to the aunties.

As Magnolia hurried to reclaim her chair, the stranger rose, the handle of his briefcase clasped in one hand. "Clarence Haddon," he said tersely. "I must speak to you in private, Ms. Willows."

"Not happening," Chandler said flatly. The aunties signaled their approval with nods and taut smiles. Haddon did not so much as look at him.

"I—I think my brother should be here," Bethany said, lifting her chin. She glanced at the aunties, who rose as one. Nodding, they hurried from the room, ostensibly to notify Garrett. Chandler stayed right where he was.

The lawyer abruptly sat down again and brought his brief-case to his knees. Extracting a sheaf of papers, he thrust them at Bethany. She gingerly took them and scanned down the first page as Haddon smoothly stated, "As you can see, my client has empowered me to offer you a cash settlement in return for your, shall we say, discretion."

A dull red flush crept up Bethany's throat into her cheeks. To Chandler's shock, she tossed the papers in Haddon's face, exclaiming, "Ten thousand dollars not to name Jason Widener as the father of my child!"

Jason Widener. That name emblazoned itself on Chandler's mind.

Haddon flattened the papers against the top of his brief-case, saying, "Let me remind you that a father has certain rights."

"Let me remind you," Bethany snapped, "that bigamy is illegal!"

Chandler jerked. Bigamy? It didn't take a rocket scientist to figure out Bethany's situation at that point. The poor woman had obviously fallen prey to some slick scoundrel.

"I have seen no evidence of bigamy," Haddon said with smugness.

Bethany folded her arms. "I have a signed marriage license from the state of Nevada. How's that for evidence?"

"An unrecorded marriage license is a curiosity," Haddon told her, waving a hand, "nothing more."

"What do you mean, *unrecorded?*" Bethany demanded, dropping her arms. Chandler stepped closer.

"I assure you that there is no record of a duly executed

marriage license with your name on it in the records of the state of Nevada."

"That's impossible!" Bethany exclaimed. "I have the license!"

"Signed by whom?"

"Myself and Jay Carter."

Jay Carter? Chandler thought. *Who was Jay Carter?*

"And did you receive that license in the mail or take it with you after the ceremony?" Haddon asked slyly.

Bethany frowned. "I think we took it with us."

"Then the license could not have been submitted for registration, could it?"

Chandler wanted to hit something. He had been surprised himself, upon signing as a witness for his sister and Stephen, to hear that the license had to be returned to the state. Only after it was recorded and stamped would it be surrendered to them. "Jay Carter obviously planned his scam very carefully."

"Perhaps," Haddon said. "I couldn't say. My client is Jason Widener."

"They're the same man!" Bethany exclaimed, tossing her arms wide.

Haddon looked her squarely in the eye. "Prove it."

The color drained from Bethany's face.

"If they weren't the same, Widener wouldn't be willing to pay her hush money," Chandler pointed out.

"Jason Widener is a wealthy, prominent man with the means to prevent unwarranted challenges to his reputation," Haddon said calmly. "It's done all the time."

"Unwarranted!" Bethany exclaimed.

"Were he the father of your child," Haddon continued, just as if she hadn't spoken, "he would certainly have the means to claim his full parental rights."

Chandler knew a threat when he heard one. So did Bethany.

She stepped back as if from a coiled rattlesnake. Impotent anger filled him. He knew that she was weighing the threat that Jason Widener would attempt to take her child from her if she so much as whispered his name in public.

Just how much more would this villain take from her? He couldn't be satisfied with her heart, her self-respect, her dignity? He had to threaten her child, too?

Oh, Lord, please help her, he thought. And then it hit him. God had helped her. He'd sent her to the Chatams, to one Chatam in particular, to *him*.

While Chandler was grappling with that, Bethany softly said, "I have no intention of claiming that Jason Widener is the father of my child and never did."

Haddon lifted an eyebrow, as if to say that was not quite sufficient.

Bethany swallowed, dropped her gaze and said, "Because he is not the father of my child."

"So who is?" Haddon pressed, clearly intent on a complete denial. "This imaginary Jay Carter you speak of?"

Imaginary? Chandler felt his hands coil into fists, but this snake was not the one that deserved the beating. Hurried footsteps sounded in the background, but Chandler was too angry to pay them much mind, too focused on Bethany and her misery.

She dropped her gaze, whispering, "I don't know who the father of my child is."

It was total humiliation, and Chandler could not bear it.

"That's a lie," he said, jolted by the sound of his own voice. The next words, however, were completely intentional. "*I* am the father of this child."

Oddly, it was a relief to say it, even if it wasn't, strictly speaking, true. A father could be a father by choice, though, he told himself.

It was impossible to say who was more startled, Haddon or Bethany.

Haddon blinked. "You're not Garrett Willows?"

"I'm Chandler Chatam," he said, "and you are leaving." Striding forward, he reached down and hauled Clarence Haddon to his feet.

"Ch-Chatam?"

"That's right." Chandler smiled, relishing the power of the Chatam name as never before. "You can tell your client that if he knows what's good for him he'll leave us alone. We don't ever want to hear from him—or you—again. Now, get out."

Clasping briefcase and papers to his chest, Haddon beat a hasty retreat.

Chandler sighed, feeling better than he had in some time, and turned to Bethany. She stood with both hands clasped to her head as if to prevent it from exploding. Beside her stood her brother, arms folded, rage snapping in his electric blue eyes.

"You're the father, after all?" he yelled, glaring at Chandler.

Chandler winced, realizing what Garrett must have heard—and, thankfully, what he hadn't heard. Suddenly, the aunts were in the room, and everyone was talking at once.

After several moments of chaos, Chandler roared, "We're getting married!"

It was like shutting off the radio. Instant silence.

Chandler parked his hands at his waist, defiantly adding, "That's all anyone needs to know."

Suddenly, Odelia rushed forward, hanky waving. "I told you! I told you! How wonderful!"

At the same time, Garrett's face cleared and his arms dropped. "Really?" he said to Bethany. "You're getting married?"

"Of course we are," Chandler replied for her, catching Odelia as she threw her arms around him in a congratulatory hug. "That's what people having babies do."

Hypatia beamed, her glowing amber eyes telling him that, while she didn't know the details, she knew exactly what he was doing and approved wholeheartedly. Mags just smiled, then broke out laughing in wonder.

Only Bethany stood like a statue, her mouth ajar. After a moment, she began to shake her head, but he knew that marrying her was the only thing to do, the right thing to do, and exactly what he wanted to do.

Now all he had to do was convince Bethany.

"You've got to be kidding." It came out as a mere whisper, her expression one of disbelief. He could not have meant what he'd said. Yes, everyone assumed that they were a couple, but… She shook her head. "You've got to be kidding me."

Taking her by the shoulders, he bodily turned her before wrapping his arm about her waist and walking her right past her brother and his aunts, through the foyer and into the library. It was one of Bethany's favorite places, a handsome, spacious room, with rich furnishings, a beverage bar and walls of books. She walked through it numbly. A lovely, quiet, very private study opened off the far corner, and that was where Chandler took her now, guiding her straight to the massive Victorian walnut partner's desk. Spinning her to face him, he placed his hands atop her shoulders and looked down into her face, his expression intense.

"This marriage is best for all of us. Think about it," he urged. "My own father believes that this child is mine. And he's not alone. Your brother even believes it now. The doctors and nurses at the hospital, everyone at church thinks that this child is mine. At least, they assume that we're married, too. So, okay. Maybe God is trying to tell us something here." He dropped a hand to the side of her stomach. It radiated warmth and strength. "Maybe I *should* be this little boy's father."

Bethany shook her head. He couldn't have thought this through. "Do you have any idea what you're saying?"

Chandler backed off a step then, his hand going to the back of his neck. "Oh, yeah." He huffed out a breath. "But, look, I've always wanted a son, and he needs a father, a real father. Seems like I'm elected." He spread his hands. "Okay, I'm not much of a bargain, I know, but better me than Jason 'Jay Carter' Widener. Bigamist."

"No kidding," she concurred, blushing to the roots of her hair. She'd hoped that he would never know what a fool she'd been.

"Bethany, look," he said, moving closer again. "No one has to know that we haven't been married all along. Well, no one who doesn't already know."

And those few were not likely to say anything, Bethany realized. Still… "I won't ask anyone to lie for me."

"Of course not. I wouldn't suggest such a thing, but if we marry quietly and just don't broadcast the date…" He shrugged.

Bethany bit her lip, trying to think it through, but her mind was whirling like a tornado. She managed to snatch one thought out of the swirl, an important one.

"Chandler, do you *want* to marry me?"

He took his time formulating his reply. "Bethany, right now I can't afford a wife and child, frankly, but I think we're supposed to do this, and if we are supposed to do it, then God will work it out, and in the meantime, that little boy is safe from a man who is *not* his father and doesn't want to be. I at least want to be his dad."

"Matthew," she whispered, her throat clogged with disappointment. Oh, what a fool she truly was! "His name is Matthew."

Chandler's gaze dropped to her middle, and he swallowed. "Matthew," he said. "I like that."

"W-we still need a middle name," she told him inanely, blinking back tears.

"How about Chandler?" he suggested hopefully, lifting his gaze to hers. "Matthew Chandler Chatam. Has a nice ring to it."

That was when she began to cry, big, splashy tears flooding her cheeks.

"Hey, look," he said quickly, "I get that your first stab at marriage didn't turn out so well for you, but you know exactly what you're getting into here. This is to protect Matthew. All this means is that Widener will have to come through me to get to him. Not that he will. Why would he? He wants to keep you from naming you as the father. Okay. Name me. But for my sake, let me be Matthew's married dad, not his unmarried dad."

"So it would be a marriage in name only," she surmised dully. Of course. What else could it be?

Blinking, Chandler shifted his weight. After a moment, he said, "B-but not forever."

She sobbed, no longer sure why she was crying now. Her gratitude was all mixed up with her admiration of this man and her stupidly breaking heart. Had she really, in some secret part of her brain, thought he might come to care for her?

He rushed on. "What I mean is, we can separate quietly later when…" The words tailed off.

Feeling weak suddenly, Bethany sagged against the edge of the desk and tried to get hold of her rioting emotions.

What difference did it make that he didn't want her? He wanted her son, and she would be selfish beyond bearing if she didn't grab such a father for her little boy. God might well have brought them here for this very reason. Where was her faith?

Keeping her gaze averted, she began drying her cheeks. "All right. When d-do you w-want to do it?"

"You mean you'll marry me?"

She nodded, unable to say more.

He leaned forward at the waist and braced his hands on his thighs, gasping as if he'd just finished a footrace.

"Whew! Wild, huh?"

Watery laughter startled out of her. "No kidding."

He laughed. Laughed. Then he straightened and strode for the door, saying, "I'd better get on this. The sooner the better, right?"

"Guess so," Bethany murmured as he left the room.

She glanced around the study, taking in the warm oak paneling, the sheltered window seat, the lovely old paintings, the antique armchairs and handsome grandfather clock. All was exactly as it should be.

And yet, everything was different.

She was getting married. Again. This time for real. And yet, not.

She shook her head, tears starting again. That seemed to be her particular talent, making marriages that were not quite real. At least this time, she knew it up front.

They married the following Friday in the office of a Justice of the Peace in Lawton, Oklahoma. Chandler wore his best boots and a brown felt hat, his darkest blue jeans, a white shirt piped in navy and a brown tie and matching Western-styled sport coat. Bethany chose a knit jumper the same shade as her blue eyes and a ruffled white blouse with white sandals.

Chandler had called his cousin Asher for a legal opinion. After determining that Bethany's situation presented no impediment, Ash had advised that Oklahoma required no residency, no blood tests and no waiting period. Because Chandler had to be there anyway to compete, the situation seemed tailor-made. They slipped out of the house before daybreak, picked up the horses and made the four-hour drive up to Lawton. Along the way, they stopped off at a discount jeweler's and purchased matching gold wedding bands.

It wasn't much of a ceremony, just Chandler, Bethany, the JP and a doddering female clerk. Bethany's hands trembled so violently when she slipped his ring onto his finger that she almost dropped it, and then she flinched when he kissed her so that it wasn't a real kiss at all, landing as much on her cheek as her lips.

He told himself that he shouldn't have expected otherwise. She'd made her wishes concerning this marriage abundantly clear. Much to his disappointment. Nevertheless, he remained convinced that, even if temporary, this marriage was best for everyone, him, Bethany, the baby and their respective families.

It was just after two o'clock in the afternoon when Chandler helped his new wife up into the passenger seat of the truck. He loosened his tie as he slid behind the steering wheel, asking, "Hungry?"

"Starved, actually," she answered.

"We'll grab something on our way to the motel." He started the engine. "We should call my aunts as soon as we get there, though I imagine they've figured out what's going on by now."

"Yes, I imagine they have. Garrett, too."

Chandler nodded. "Once I eat, I've got to change and get to the arena to check on the horses and meet Drew." As soon as they'd arrived in Lawton, they'd gone to the arena and dropped off the horses and trailer. He'd arranged to meet Drew for check-in as close to three-thirty as he could manage. "You can relax at the motel until I get back," he told her.

"Could I come with you?" Bethany asked tentatively.

Chandler jerked a glance at her, surprised but pleased. He managed a nonchalant shrug. "Sure, if you want. Keep a lookout for Lee Boulevard, will you?"

Bethany nodded and dutifully began reading street signs. She spotted a drive-through that offered fried chicken dinners, so they carried that to the motel, then sat around a desk affixed to the wall in the crowded double room to eat. He made the call, speaking briefly to Hypatia, letting her know to expect them back Monday afternoon. He didn't see any reason to rush back to Buffalo Creek Sunday night. Might as well sleep in and take their time. It was their honeymoon, after all. Sort of.

He was just getting off the phone with the aunties when Bethany went into the tiny bathroom to change her clothes. While she did that, he removed his tie and coat and swapped out his boots and hat, rolling back the cuffs of his longs sleeves. Bethany emerged a few minutes later wearing a long red tunic and black leggings with tall red boots. Worn to a comfortable suppleness, they weren't cowboy boots, but they did have a Western heel.

"Is this okay? I can't get into my jeans."

"You look great," he told her honestly.

"Thanks." She wrinkled her nose and plucked at the tunic. "I used to wear this as a dress."

Chandler admitted to himself that he'd have liked to have seen that then cleared his throat and led her out of the room.

They met Drew and Cindy walking across a field where they'd parked, about a hundred yards away from the rodeo arena.

"Hey!" Chandler shook Drew's hand, smiling and nodding at Cindy, whose gaze boldly swept over Bethany.

"This is my wife, Bethany," he said, finding that the words rolled off his tongue with surprising ease. "Honey, this is my new partner, Drew Shaw, and his wife, Cindy."

Drew's jaw was hanging open. He recovered and doffed his hat just as Cindy launched herself forward and dealt Chandler a stinging slap on the upper arm.

"You rat! You never said anything about being married and having a kid on the way! What's wrong with you?"

Before Chandler could stammer a reply to that, Bethany came to his rescue. "Men! They think we know everything that goes through their heads, even when they're as private as this one." She gave Chandler a little pat on the chest. He thought his shirt buttons might just pop, his heart swelled so.

Drew chuckled, shaking his head. "Man, you could've saved me a lot of headache if you'd just brought your woman around sooner."

"What do you mean?" Bethany asked.

"I mean, Cindy might not have worried so much about the two of us partnering up if she'd known he was married. In her words, she doesn't want me 'hanging around with some chick magnet' while she's stuck at home with the baby."

Chandler laughed. "No chance of that here."

"Oh, please," Bethany said in a scoffing tone. "If ever there was a chick magnet…" She broke off, color blooming in her cheeks.

Chandler grinned. He supposed he'd drawn his fair share of female attention, but he'd stopped paying attention to the buckle bunnies that came around a long time ago. Too many party girls more interested in the party than a guy holding out for something serious when the time was right.

The time wasn't right, not by Chandler's reckoning, but "something serious" had blindsided him anyway. He guessed it happened like that a lot. Too often, though, what blindsided a fellow turned into a hit-and-run. His heart didn't just slow at that thought, it all but stopped.

"That's what wives are for," Cindy was saying, "to keep the chicks away. Right?" She winked at Bethany, asking, "So when are you due?"

"October eighteenth."

Cindy patted her baby bump. "This one won't show up until the first of November."

"He," Drew said, grinning. "It's a boy."

"No kidding?" Chandler laughed at himself, that being one of Bethany's favorite phrases. She was rubbing off on him already, this new wife of his. "Ours, too."

"That's cool," Drew said. "Who knows? Maybe one day our sons will be roping partners."

Something lurched inside Chandler, and he felt the warm glow of fatherly pride. Whatever happened with him and Bethany, he told himself, he'd always have Matthew, at least. If that didn't seem like quite enough just now, well, he'd have to leave that to God.

Chapter Eight

*O*urs, *too.*

Those simple words had echoed in Bethany's head from the instant that Chandler had spoken them. They raised goose bumps on her skin and plucked at her heartstrings.

Our child. Mine and now Chandler's.

The momentous ramifications weighed on her, filling her with equal parts joy and concern.

The air unit kicked on, filling the dark room with its rattling hum. Chandler rolled over again on the other bed. Apparently, he was having as much trouble getting to sleep as she was. She couldn't forget that this was their wedding night or that Chandler had offered to get separate rooms instead of just separate beds for them.

Knowing that money was a concern for him, she had insisted that this would be fine. Besides, if anyone should come looking for him, it would look decidedly odd if they weren't together. The main reason, however, was that she simply hadn't wanted to be alone on this of all nights. It didn't change anything, of course. This marriage was still a sham. At least it was a legal sham. She told herself that was a step forward, but it didn't feel that way. It felt…lonely.

Chandler shifted again and punched his pillow into a more

pleasing shape. She suspected that part of his restlessness had to do with the fact that he slept—or tried to sleep—fully clothed in jeans and a T-shirt. Another reason probably had to do with his performance that night.

He and Drew were leading the team roping, though two more go-rounds of competition remained before overall winners could be determined. Drew was in first place in his personal event, too, while Chandler had come in ahead in the steer wrestling and second in the tie down.

Bethany hadn't been able to watch the steer wrestling, not after the first competitor. If anyone had told her that she'd wind up married to a man who did something so dangerous as throw himself off a running horse onto the horns of a stampeding steer, she wouldn't have believed it, and she dared not dwell on it now.

To distract herself, she asked into the silence, "Do you ever hear the air conditioner at Chatam House?"

Chandler pushed up onto one elbow. From her bed, she could just make out the shape of his head in the darkened room. "Nope. Never do."

"Isn't it right above us in the attic there?" she mused. "I think that's what Magnolia said, that they put the central air units in the attic."

Chandler collapsed back onto his pillow. "Yep. Air units are in the attic."

"Thought so."

For a long moment, only the hum of the fan blowing cold air into the room filled the silence. It occurred to Bethany that she had been remiss, and this was as good a time as any to say what should have been said earlier.

"Chandler."

"Hmm?"

"Thank you. For everything. For offering me a ride back there in that diner. For introducing me to your dad and driving me around. For rushing me to the emergency room and not embarrassing me that day in church. For throwing Jay's lawyer out of the house. Most of all, for claiming Matthew."

Matthew. Not her. He hadn't claimed her, even if she was his wife, but she couldn't let that matter.

She sat up, aware that her white sleep shirt and baggy shorts made her more visible than him.

"You'll be an awesome dad," she said, knowing in her heart that it was true.

Chandler slid his hands behind his head. "I did this as much for me as anyone else," he muttered at the ceiling.

She was glad that his reputation was safe now, glad that she could do that much for him, at least. God above knew that he deserved it, that and more.

"You don't owe me any thanks, Bethany," he went on. "You're sharing your son with me. There's not much greater gift than that."

Bethany smiled, feeling as though her heart smiled, too. "I prayed that my child would have an awesome dad, you know. I just didn't think it would be you."

"Who would?" he retorted wryly.

She could have argued that point but feared giving away too much of her feelings. Instead, she changed the subject.

"Speaking of awesome," she said, injecting a note of fun into her voice. "I have never seen anything like what you did today. I had no idea anyone could move that fast or that accurately. And the horses! Oh, my goodness. How long did you have to train them? Cindy says you're a 'dab hand,' by the way."

Chandler chuckled. "Not sure what that means, frankly, but I've been working with this bunch for years."

He talked about the horses for a while. Ginger Boy was eight years old and had been with him almost the whole time. He'd had Red Rover, a nine-year-old, for only five years.

"Arroyo," he went on, "is the old man, nearly seventeen. We've been together the better part of a decade. He was the first horse I bought on my own. As for Ébano, he's the youngster at six, and I've only worked with him about a year. He'd been through a few hands before I got him, and nobody had really pegged him as a roping horse, but I think we can win together. He's got good bloodlines and a natural talent, even if he is a bit high-strung, which is why I got him at a good price of ten thousand."

"Ten thousand dollars?" she exclaimed.

He turned his head, targeting her form in the dark. "That's a tenth of what a good roping horse can cost. I figure he's really worth seven or eight times that. Like I said, he's got fine bloodlines."

"Kind of like you," she mumbled around a yawn, stretching out on her bed again.

"Can't take any credit for that," Chandler said softly. "That's just pure blessing, being a Chatam."

"Yes, I know." She yawned again, feeling pleasantly tired now. "Thank you," she said again some minutes later, thinking that she and Matthew were Chatams now, too. The words whispered out on a sigh.

Pure blessing, he'd said, and he was certainly right about that.

It was her last thought before sleep finally claimed her.

Listening to the soft, even breathing of his wife, Chandler rolled onto his side and stared through the darkness at the white figure on the other bed.

Some wedding night, he mused. Some wedding. Come to that, it was some marriage.

At least it was legal.

He couldn't help wondering now what it was going to cost him, though. He'd been so worried about finances that he hadn't stopped to worry about any other sort of cost. Now, he knew that he was in serious danger of losing his heart.

Being with her tonight, introducing her as his wife, knowing she was up there in the stands watching him, it had all felt so right. She had even cemented his partnership with Drew, which felt more like friendship now, rather than just a business arrangement. It would likely be more permanent than this marriage.

He wished that their marriage was more than just a convenient, temporary agreement, but it did have its benefits. Having Bethany on his arm would make any man proud. And how many men could choose their sons? Funny, though, that his reputation didn't seem so important now. Why should it? He'd been letting Kreger drag it through the mud for years, after all. Still, he didn't want to be thought of as the sort of man who would impregnate a woman outside of the bonds of marriage, especially not as the sort of man who would do that and then abandon the mother of his child, not to mention the child himself. Yes, this marriage did have benefits for him.

His main concerns were Bethany and Matthew, however. Maybe it wasn't much of a marriage, but it was a marriage to a Chatam. He had given them both that much.

Chatams were godly, loving people, and they took care of their own. He had no doubt that his father, sister, brothers, aunts, uncles, cousins, every last member of the family, would accept and love his wife and son, even if some of them would be less than pleased with him once word of this marriage got out.

The aunts would stand by him, though. He had no doubt of that. He smiled, grateful and glad.

Bethany was right. He did have an excellent pedigree. That, he realized, was one of the greatest blessings of his life. It was about time that he started living up to those bloodlines.

An Important Message from the Editors of Love Inspired Books

Dear Reader,

We hope you've enjoyed reading this heart-warming romance novel. If you would like to receive more of these great stories delivered directly to your door, we're offering to send you <u>two more</u> of the books you love so much, **plus** two exciting Mystery gifts— absolutely <u>FREE</u>!

Please enjoy them with our compliments...

Jean Gordon

Editor,
Love Inspired®

Peel off seal and place inside...

EDITORS "FREE GIFTS" SEAL · THANK YOU

(LI-EC-10R)

HOW TO VALIDATE YOUR
EDITOR'S FREE GIFTS!
"THANK YOU"

1   Peel off the FREE GIFTS SEAL from front cover. Place it in the space provided at right. This automatically entitles you to receive two free books and two exciting surprise gifts.

2   Send back this card and you'll get 2 Love Inspired® books. These books have a combined cover price of $11.00 for the regular-print and $12.50 for the larger-print in the U.S. and $13.00 for the regular-print or $14.50 for the larger-print in Canada, but they are yours to keep absolutely FREE!

3   There's no catch. You're under no obligation to buy anything. We charge nothing—ZERO—for your first shipment. And you don't have to make any minimum number of purchases—not even one!

4   We call this line Love Inspired because every month you'll receive books that are filled with joy, faith and traditional values. The stories will lift your spirit and warm your heart! You'll like the convenience of getting them delivered to your home well before they are in stores. And you'll love our discount prices, too!

5   We hope that after receiving your free books you'll want to remain a subscriber. But the choice is yours—to continue or cancel, anytime at all! So why not take us up on our invitation, with no risk of any kind. You'll be glad you did!

6   And remember...just for validating your Editor's Free Gifts Offer, we'll send you 2 books and 2 gifts, *ABSOLUTELY FREE!*

YOURS FREE!
We'll send you two fabulous surprise gifts (worth about $10) absolutely FREE, simply for accepting our no-risk offer!

Steeple
Hill®

The Editor's "Thank You" Free Gifts Include:

- Two inspirational romance books
- Two exciting surprise gifts

YES!

PLACE FREE GIFTS SEAL HERE

I have placed my Editor's "thank you" Free Gifts seal in the space provided above. Please send me the 2 FREE books and 2 FREE gifts for which I qualify. I understand that I am under no obligation to purchase anything further, as explained on the opposite page.

About how many NEW paperback fiction books have you purchased in the past 3 months?

❏ 0-2   ❏ 3-6   ❏ 7 or more
E5SW   **E5S9**   **E5TL**

❏ I prefer the regular-print edition   ❏ I prefer the larger-print edition
105/305 IDL   **122/322 IDL**

Please Print

FIRST NAME

LAST NAME

ADDRESS

APT.#   CITY

STATE/PROV.   ZIP/POSTAL CODE

Thank You, Lord, he began in silence, *for letting me be born a Chatam.*

He had much else for which to be thankful, too, so much that he felt himself sinking into sleep before he could get through the mental list. He struggled to stay with it, but sleep finally pulled him into dreams. Even from there, he reached out instinctively to God, until he at last knew peace.

"My sister's here," Chandler announced as soon as the truck turned up the drive early that next Monday afternoon. He nodded toward a small red convertible parked in front of the mansion.

Bethany sat up a little straighter, one hand going to her hair, which she'd slapped up in a messy ponytail bun. She felt tired and grimy after the trip back from Lawton this morning and all that went with dropping off the horses again, not that Chandler had let her help with that. He wouldn't even let her get out of the truck for fear that the horses would bump into her. She supposed he was right about that, but she so wanted to be as much a partner to him as Drew was, as much a partner as Cindy was to her husband.

Of course, the Shaws' marriage was real.

The rodeo had fascinated and frightened her, though she'd done her best to hide the latter from Chandler. The roping was all skill, but the steer wrestling… Chandler was bummed because he'd finished out of the money in his personal events that weekend, but at least he and Drew had taken second place in the team roping, which seemed to please Drew. Chandler, however, appeared to feel that he'd somehow let down the team. Bethany hoped that seeing his sister would perk him up.

The aunts had told her a lot about Kaylie and her husband, Stephen. Chandler had also spoken of his younger sister with great affection, which Bethany felt was surely mutual.

Whether that affection would extend to the pregnant woman who was now his wife, Bethany didn't know. In truth, she couldn't think of any reason why it should.

Chandler brought the truck to a stop in front of the house and came around to take Bethany's arm as she slid out on her side. He escorted her up the steps and across the porch to the door, where he paused, lifted his eyebrows and said, "Here we go."

They'd already discussed what sort of reception they could expect from his aunts and her brother. Kaylie presented a complete unknown. Bethany sucked in a deep breath, and Chandler opened the door.

"Surprise!"

Odelia rushed forward, waving her hankie wildly. She wore tiers of bloodred lace and rubies the size of robin eggs on her earlobes, hopefully fake ones. A petite, big-eyed young woman with long, soft sandy-red hair watched calmly from the center of the foyer as Odelia hugged first Bethany and then Chandler, babbling about shopping and cakes and honeymoons.

"And look!" she exclaimed, waving her hankie at the young woman, who wore a chic sleeveless sheath of crisp lilac linen, her hair held back by a matching headband. "Look who just showed up!"

Bethany shrank inwardly, rooted to the floor in her flip-flops, bagged out navy leggings and a clownish polka-dotted top that she'd found on clearance at the discount store. She had never felt less attractive.

"Kaylie," Chandler said, slipping away from Bethany to hug his sister. "Welcome home. Is Stephen here?"

"No. And don't change the subject."

"Which is?"

Drawing back from the embrace, Kaylie tilted her head and lifted her eyebrows at her brother before looking pointedly to Bethany. Then she balled up her fist and punched him in the gut. The blow didn't so much as rock him, but he caved belatedly and let out a long-suffering sigh. Odelia giggled uncertainly.

"You could've told me," Kaylie accused before abruptly shooting Bethany an apologetic glance. "I didn't even know he was seeing anyone, let alone married!"

Chandler seemed to struggle for an explanation before he finally said, "We decided for our own reasons to keep it quiet."

Kaylie turned to Bethany, saying sweetly, "Hello. I'm Kaylie."

Bethany trilled her fingers in a hesitant wave. "Bethany. Pleased to meet you."

"Come, come!" tittered Odelia, waving them all toward the parlor. "Come and see!"

Kaylie tossed a look at Chandler as she moved to follow her aunt, muttering, "You're lucky that was my fist and not Stephen's."

Chandler sighed again and rolled his eyes, holding out his hand to Bethany. She went to him gratefully. Together they entered the parlor.

"Surprise!"

This time it was a group effort. The aunties stood around a tea trolley laden with a white cake decorated with spun, sugar roses and the words "Congratulations, Bethany and Chandler." It looked for all the world like a single-layer wedding cake. Thankfully, it bore nothing so incriminating as bells or a tiny statue of a bride and groom. The cake in itself would have been surprise enough; add Garrett and the rest of the staff along with an entire shop full of baby goods, and the effect was simply stunning.

Beside her, Chandler seemed every bit as staggered as

Bethany was by the goods crammed into the room. He lifted his hands, palms out, as if to say, "What happened?"

With a glance in Kaylie's direction, Hypatia answered the unasked question. "We went shopping for the baby. The, ah, cake was Hilda's idea."

"Oooh," Bethany said, spying a beautiful spooled crib. That was for her baby? She rushed toward it, unable to help herself.

The aunts had outfitted the antique reproduction with a blue, yellow and green patchwork quilt, pale blue sheets and matching tailored bed skirt. In addition, it was filled with stuffed animals and tiny clothes.

"Oh, look!" There was a neat little sailor suit spread across a teensy pillow and next to that a wee pair of blue jeans and color-blocked, Western-style shirt.

Chandler nudged a stuffed horse on wheels with one booted toe. "First mount," he said with a chuckle.

All in all, there was more paraphernalia than Bethany could ever have imagined. She'd pictured a secondhand bassinet, a few glass bottles and a small layette, and here was everything they could possibly need!

Chandler stood in the midst of it all and spread his arms, saying to his aunts, "You know you've gone way overboard."

"Oh, but we had such fun," Hypatia said dismissively, waving them over to the tea cart with a regal roll of her hand. "Come now and cut the cake."

Hilda, her thin, straight, gray-and-gold hair tucked behind her ears, produced an elegant silver server, smiling so widely that her double chins almost wreathed her face. Her husband, Chester, dressed in his usual short-sleeved white shirt and black slacks with black suspenders, produced a camera and focused it at the tea trolley, while Hilda's sister Carol, her dull blond hair wrapped around her head in a thin braid, hurried to take small china dessert plates from beneath the cart.

Chandler looked at Bethany and held out his hand, one eyebrow arched. Smiling, she went to him and together they moved behind the tea trolley. Hilda turned over the silver cake server. Bethany gripped it. Grinning, Chandler wrapped his big hand around hers, and they posed for the camera. They cut the first piece of the single layer, then laughingly carved out two more while Chester continued to snap photos. These first pieces were served to the aunties. A piece for Kaylie followed, then those for Garrett and the staff. Finally, they cut a piece to share.

Carol handed them two forks, and for a moment, they stood there staring at each other. Chandler's gaze slid to his sister. Then he looked back to Bethany, cut off a bite and fed it to her. With Kaylie there it was foolish, but Bethany couldn't resist indulging in this one minor wedding ritual. She mirrored Chandler's actions. He was smiling when he started to chew. Then suddenly he snatched the plate from Bethany's hand and pretended to hold her off while gobbling it down. Everyone laughed. Immediately, Hilda took up the server to plop another piece onto an empty china plate and shove it into Bethany's hands.

She no longer cared what she looked like in her well-worn clothes and messy bun with her pregnant belly sticking out. She was at her husband's side, celebrating their marriage and coming child among friends and family. It occurred to her suddenly that these dear old ladies were now her aunts as well as Chandler's and, by extension, Matthew's. That, too, was reason to celebrate.

When Kaylie sought her out a little later, Bethany allowed herself to be pulled aside with only a hint of trepidation.

"It's belated, but welcome to the family," she said.

"Thank you."

"I'm stunned, of course. This is so unlike Chandler. I mean, to marry in secret without telling anyone, and then to present us with baby and bride at once."

"I-It's not what you think," Bethany began, swamped with guilt, but Chandler was suddenly at her side, his arm sliding about her shoulders.

"It is what it is," he stated defensively. "It's not like I need the family's approval to marry."

"Of course not," Kaylie said. "But what about Dad? He's going to be hurt because you didn't let him perform the ceremony and because you didn't tell him the truth when you first introduced him to Bethany."

Chandler bowed his head. "It wasn't my intention to hurt Dad, and he didn't exactly give me a chance to explain anything. He just jumped to the worst possible conclusions about me."

Kaylie threw up her hands. "So you didn't tell him that you were married? Yeah, that makes perfect sense."

"This is ridiculous," Bethany muttered. Surely, they could trust his sister and the rest of the family with the truth. "We were only ma—"

"Doing what was best for us," Chandler interrupted, clamping her tightly against his side. "If Dad can't accept that, it's his problem."

Kaylie sighed. "I'm not saying he was right to jump to conclusions, but it wouldn't have killed you to do the right thing even if he didn't."

"Chandler *always* does the right thing," Bethany declared, frowning. "You should know that."

Kaylie blinked at her. And then she beamed. "Yes. You're right." She turned her smile on her brother. "He does always do the right thing. Eventually."

"You three come have some tea," Hypatia called just then, having seated herself in her favorite chair.

"Yes, ma'am," Kaylie replied. She quickly leaned in and kissed Bethany's cheek, then patted her brother's and walked back to join the party, smiling.

Chandler kept his arm about Bethany's shoulders until his sister was out of earshot. Then he put his forehead to Bethany's, lifted a hand to her belly and softly said, "This is my son, mine and yours. That's what we agreed and that's all anyone needs to know. Right? When and where we married is no one else's business."

"You can't blame me for not wanting her to think badly of you," Bethany argued softly. "She thinks you lied to your father about being married!"

"All that matters is that you're now my wife," he whispered, "the mother of *my* child, and what's best for the two of you takes precedent over everything else. Besides, Kaylie's too sweet to think badly of anyone, least of all one of her brothers."

Bethany sighed. She hated that no one else really knew what a selfless, caring thing he had done. He wrapped his arms around her and hugged her tight. Bethany closed her eyes, wishing that this marriage wasn't just a convenient arrangement. She wanted a real marriage and real love with a real man. Like Chandler.

Hypatia called them again, and they broke apart to eat more cake and drink cups of tea, herbal in Bethany's case, in secret celebration of a marriage that really wasn't. Why, Bethany wondered, did that always seem to be the case where she was concerned?

A wedding, Chandler told himself again, *deserved to be celebrated, even if it had to be celebrated in secret,* and he blessed the aunties for seeing to it. He was glad that his sister had wandered into the midst of the thing, too, even if it had caused some uncomfortable moments. He hated not telling her the whole truth, especially because it seemed to pain Bethany, but the more people who knew, the greater the chance that Matthew's parentage would be questioned. Chandler wasn't worried about Widener. The man would be a fool to inject himself into the situation at this point. Bethany, on the other hand, could be publicly embarrassed without the names Widener or Carter ever coming into it, and that Chandler could not abide.

Still, Kaylie was his sister, one of the people who loved him most in this world, and she would never knowingly do anything to hurt him or anyone else. That was the very thought in his mind when Bethany yawned behind her hand and excused herself before heading upstairs for a nap.

"I'll bring all this stuff up later," Chandler told her, and Garrett promised to help.

"I should be going, too," Kaylie said, getting to her feet. "Stephen and Dad will be wondering what happened to me. Walk me out," she said to Chandler.

He cast a glance at the aunties before following his sister out into the foyer. She turned on him at once, whispering, "You don't fool me, Chandler Chatam."

Alarmed, he took her arm and steered her into the library, closing the door behind them.

"You just married that girl," she went on. "I don't know why you waited. Maybe you didn't know about the baby until recently. Maybe you had to be sure that you were the father."

He looked her straight in the eye and said, "I *am* that baby's father, and I don't want anyone thinking otherwise."

"Oh, Chandler." She hugged him. "Of course you're the baby's father." She pulled back and framed his face with her hands. "And you obviously adore Bethany and your son."

He didn't know what to say to that, except, "I—I just want to do what's best for them."

"Naturally. Whatever held you two back, I'm glad you worked it out because she's obviously head over heels for you, too."

He'd have laughed at that—if it hadn't hurt so unexpectedly to know that Kaylie was wrong about Bethany's feelings.

"'Chandler *always* does the right thing,'" Kaylie mimicked dreamily. "No wonder you love her so much. She thinks you hung the moon."

Love Bethany? Even as his heart clunked inside his chest, he opened his mouth to deny it, but then he clamped his lips shut again. What kind of an idiot denied loving his own wife? Besides, he wasn't entirely sure that he didn't love Bethany. On some level.

Oh, who was he kidding. He was crazy about her. Not that it made one whit of difference. The marriage was what it was, what they had agreed to.

"I—I'm sorry about Dad," he said truthfully, turning the conversation away from his feelings for Bethany and hers for him, or her lack of them.

"I know," Kaylie said, "and don't worry. Your secret's safe with me. You've done the right thing, and that's what matters most."

"I'm not asking you to lie to anyone," he pointed out, mentally squirming.

She waved a hand as she got to her feet. "Of course not, but whenever anyone asks me when and where you got married, I'll simply say that I'm not sure of the date, which is the absolute truth. You eloped, with none of the family the wiser. I'll have to tell the rest of the family that you and Bethany are married, though, especially Dad."

Chandler shrugged. "I never intended to keep them in the dark indefinitely."

"Dad's going to be upset."

"So what else is new?"

She shook her head. "Chandler, you've got to make your peace with him."

"I know, I know, and I will. When the time is right."

Kaylie sighed. "I guess that will have to do. Now, I have to get home before Stephen and Dad run out of polite conversation." She promised to tell Chandler all about the trip later and hurried off saying that she was looking for a larger house to lease for the three of them while her and Stephen's new house was being built. "A *much* larger house," she said with a cheeky grin.

"Thankfully we're here with the aunties," Chandler told her with heartfelt sincerity.

She went out, chuckling. Chandler walked into the foyer to find Magnolia there, obviously waiting for him.

"I just wanted to let you know that we moved your things into the master suite," she said softly.

Chandler's eyebrows jumped up into his hairline. "What about Garrett?" How was he to share a suite with Bethany *and* her brother without letting the latter know that this marriage was not all it seemed?

"Garrett's moved back into the carriage house," Mags told Chandler. "That leaves plenty of room for the baby."

Relieved, Chandler blurted, "Thanks, but I hope we're in our own place before he's born."

"Oh, what a shame that would be," Magnolia said, all but pouting. Chandler's jaw dropped. Mags was the last one he'd have expected this from! She quickly recovered and lifted her chin, adding, "Odelia will be so disappointed."

Laughing, Chandler hugged her. "You don't fool me, you old softie."

Magnolia gave him a sheepish grin. "Having a baby around could be fun."

Chandler headed for the stairs. "I'll remind you of that when he's waking up the whole household night after night."

Suddenly he wondered if he'd lost his ever-loving mind. What did he really know about being a father or a husband? Why hadn't he just walked away? He could have at any juncture. He still could.

"I have earplugs!" Mags called after him.

He just laughed. He didn't believe for a moment that she'd use them. No more than he believed that he could ever walk away from Bethany and her, *their*, son.

Chapter Nine

Staring at the hat atop the highboy dresser and the boots arranged neatly on the floor beside it, Bethany hugged herself. Why hadn't she thought of this? Of course, the aunties and Garrett would assume that a husband and wife would share a bedroom. As far as they were concerned, this was a real marriage, a whole marriage, so naturally they'd moved Chandler's things into the master bedroom of the three-bedroom suite. Perhaps, she thought wistfully, they ought to just forget this marriage-in-name-only business and do their best to make this work, not that she had anything to say about it. This was Chandler's choice, and she had agreed. It wasn't fair to try to change things now.

She heard his footsteps in the sitting room. Funny how quickly she'd come to recognize his particular long, sure gait. Garrett's steps were quieter, quicker. *Must be the boots,* she thought, smiling.

"Don't worry," he said from the open doorway. "I'll move into one of the other bedrooms."

She turned to find him leaning a shoulder against the doorjamb. "Garrett—"

"Has moved back into the carriage house," he said quickly.

That made sense. Still…

"If you move, everyone in the house will know that we're not, um, together."

He shrugged and shook his head. "My aunts won't say anything. Not to either of us. Maybe not even to each other. Certainly not to anyone else."

She doubted that Garrett would say anything, either. The sleeping arrangements between a husband and wife were a private, matter after all.

Straightening, Chandler gave his head a jerk as he asked, "Which of the other rooms do you want to use as the nursery?"

Her hand resting automatically atop her belly, she said, "The closest one, I guess."

He looked behind him as if judging the distance between doors and nodded before moving forward into the room. Bethany stood awkwardly where she was. He came to a stop mere inches from her. Lungs seizing, she looked up hopefully. For several heartbeats, his warm brown gaze held hers. Words that she longed to say sprang to her tongue.

I don't want another sham marriage. Can't we try to make this real? Give me a chance to be the wife of your heart.

But then Chandler lifted his eyes and carefully reached around her for the hat atop the highboy. Abruptly, Jay's acidic warning drowned out her longings.

"You think any other man is going to want you with your crazy background and a kid in tow?"

Feeling foolish, she quickly moved aside.

"Only be a minute," Chandler said, bending to pick up the boots.

Nodding, she hurried out into the sitting room, leaving him to rummage through drawers in search of his things. He came out a few moments later, his arms full, and clumped across to the room Garrett had occupied. It took several more trips, but eventually he had all of his things out of her room.

"That's it," he said, disappearing through his door once more. He was back in an instant, his arms empty. "You can take your nap now."

"Thanks," she said, smiling wanly. "I will."

"I just might have a nap, too," he told her, "once I get all this stuff put away. Busy day."

She nodded. He stood there for a few moments longer, then he returned her nod, stepped back and closed his door. Bethany went into her room and did the same. It was, perhaps, the loneliest moment of her life.

After moving his things from Bethany's bedroom, Chandler virtually hid in his room. He told himself that this was far more comfortable than sharing a motel room with separate beds, but it somehow felt more private. Worse, he knew that everyone in the house thought they would be sharing that one bed and that, to his shock, embarrassed him. They were adults, after all, and she was his wife, for pity's sake. Except that she wasn't, not in every way. And she never would be.

He didn't even go down to dinner, letting everyone think that he was sleeping when what he was really doing was worrying. The cowardice of that shamed him, as it left Bethany to explain his absence. He'd heard her pause outside his door moments after Chester called them down for the evening meal, but she hadn't knocked, so he'd let her go on her way while he stayed behind to stew about things he couldn't control.

He worried about how Bethany truly felt about this marriage, if his presence in the suite would make her uncomfortable and whether he'd be able to provide her with her own home before the baby came. He pondered failure as a husband and a father, as well as in his chosen career, basically second-guessing everything in his life. Eventually, before he could drive himself completely mad, he went to his knees and found a measure of peace.

It did not come soon enough to keep him from oversleeping the next morning.

Bethany woke him at only the last possible moment. As a result, he had to dash out of the house without breakfast or a shave to get her to work on time. On the way, they briefly discussed how they were going to handle Hub and decided that they would simply present a unified front and apologize for any hurt feelings.

They barely got through the door, however, when Hubner attacked.

"You lied to me!"

Tired, heartsick and starving, Chandler felt his own temper spike, but he bit his tongue. At first.

"You *both* lied to me!" Hubner accused. "I expect it from you," he snapped at Chandler. Then he glared accusingly at Bethany. "But you, Bethany?"

"Now, wait a minute!" Chandler interrupted angrily. "Bethany did what she had to do, and you didn't believe her anyway, so what difference does it make?"

"What difference? That's my grandchild she's carrying, and she denied it to my face! How can I ever trust either of you again?"

"Think what you will of me, Dad," Chandler said, more wounded than he'd expected to be and downright furious at this criticism of Bethany. "I've made my share of mistakes. But Bethany has done nothing wrong."

Quite the opposite, in fact. She had been wronged. Even if Hubner didn't know that, this was unfair, so far as Chandler was concerned.

"Nothing?" Hub scoffed, raking her with a scathing glance.

Chandler lost it. "How dare you judge her!" he shouted. "Don't think I'll let you get away with jumping to conclusions about her! You've done that with me time and again, and I've put up with it because you're my father, but she's off-limits!"

"Okay, that's enough," Bethany interjected calmly. "I'll take it from here, thank you." Going up on tiptoe, she kissed Chandler on the cheek. Then she lifted both hands and literally shoved him backward out the door, which she pulled closed firmly behind him.

That kiss threw him off balance to the point that a long moment passed before he fully realized what had happened.

He was reaching for the handle to go right back inside when he heard Hub say, "Bethany, I did not mean to imply... I don't know any of the details, but i-it was not my intention to insult you."

Bethany folded her arms. "No. Only to insult your son."

Chandler stepped to the side, out of sight of the glass door, curious as to what she would say next.

"You don't understand," Hub said in a morose voice. "Somehow I failed that boy. He's always done the very thing that I don't want him to do."

"He's not a disobedient boy!" Bethany pointed out. "He's a man, a very fine man, a far better man than you seem to know. Maybe he's not perfect, but who is? At least he always does what he believes best, though no one seems to give him credit for that."

"What he thinks best is too often *not!*" Hub argued.

"In your opinion. Okay, so you sometimes disagree. So what? Why can't you see past that to the man he is? Sure, he's made some mistakes. Everyone does. But you have no reason to be disappointed with the man he has become."

"You say that because you're in love with him," Hub grumbled.

Chandler didn't realize that he was holding his breath until Bethany quietly said, "I say that because I know him."

Chandler dropped his head.

No matter what Kaylie thought, Bethany clearly was not in love with him. Why would she be? If not for the aunties, he wouldn't even be able to house and feed her. He'd let Kreger lead him around by the nose for so long that he'd completely lost his way. And he'd called that loyalty!

"He's just doing what he always does," Bethany went on, showing him real loyalty. "He's doing his best for everyone. You may not believe that, but it's the truth."

"I don't know what to believe," Hub muttered. "I just don't understand any of this."

"You could give your son the benefit of the doubt, though," Bethany told him gently. "You do everyone else."

Chandler smiled wanly. She didn't love him as he wanted her to, the way a wife usually loved her husband, but she was a good friend, good enough to defend him.

For a moment, Hub said nothing, but then he muttered, "Everyone else isn't my son."

"And that's the real problem, isn't it?" Bethany said quietly. "You judge him more harshly because he is your son."

What Hub replied, Chandler couldn't quite make out. It didn't matter, anyway. Hub would always think the worst of him. Chandler accepted that.

As for Bethany, he expected nothing more than the respect and friendship that she'd already shown him. She might have settled temporarily for a marriage with a man whom she couldn't love, but that wouldn't last. As loyal and sweet and considerate as she was, sooner or later, she'd want her freedom.

When that time came, he was honor-bound to let her go. He'd agreed to that, and he would keep his word.

But somehow, he had to manage to keep his heart in the process—even if it meant keeping his distance from this lovely and lovable wife of his.

"I'm worried about you," Garrett said, more than a week later. "I thought when you married Chandler that things would change."

Leaning forward, he braced his elbows on his knees, sitting opposite Bethany in one of a pair of antique armchairs that matched the sofa upon which she sat. Bethany leaned back into one corner of the sofa, hitched her leg up onto the seat and went about tying the shoestrings of her cheap, bright yellow tennis shoes.

"Things have changed," she told him.

Not as much as she would like, perhaps, but things had changed, and for the better. She no longer had to worry about Jay or, rather, Jason. She need not fear being thought of as an unwed mother and all that implied. As Mrs. Chandler Chatam, she could hold her head up high and finally put the past behind her. Best of all, Matthew had a father who wanted him. How could she complain about any of that—or expect more? So what if her husband had ignored her for the past week and more?

It hurt, that was what, and she had to do something to change it.

"You shouldn't be working," Garrett said. "You're not well."

"I'm fine," she told him, keeping her gaze averted as she shifted sides and hitched up the other leg. "Pregnancy is not a disease, you know, and I like my job."

In truth, the work did not overtire her, but her cramps had

gradually returned. Still, that didn't bother her nearly as much as Chandler did.

He had barely spoken to her lately. Even when he'd driven her to and from work, he hadn't really been there, and now he was heading out to another rodeo without even telling her goodbye. She'd heard him head downstairs just moments ago, and she wanted to catch up with him before he left.

Suddenly the door opened, and Chandler rushed through it.

"Thank goodness you're dressed," he said, a harried look on his unshaven face. "I was climbing in the truck when I realized that I couldn't go off without you, but hurry, please."

Thrilled, Bethany got to her feet, tugging on the bottom of the rainbow-striped tunic top that she wore tied at the shoulders over an old blue T-shirt and a pair of matching leggings, both of which had faded to a pale denim shade.

"Wait just a minute, and I'll throw—"

"Now, Bethany, please," Chandler interrupted. "I'll explain on the way." Turning, he went out again.

Glancing toward the bedroom, she shrugged. She'd go without luggage if she had to. She would gladly dip into her savings to buy a change of clothes, she was that pleased to be going with her husband. Calling out a hasty farewell to her brother, Bethany grabbed her handbag from the desk beside the door and followed Chandler toward the stairs. He was halfway down the landing when she called out, "What's the hurry?"

"I have to be somewhere before seven-thirty."

"Oh. Okay."

"I'll bring the truck around front," he told her, sprinting ahead down the stairs.

Bethany kept a more sedate pace, aware that her center of gravity had shifted forward and that a fall could be catastrophic. The truck was waiting at the end of the brick walkway when she got there. She hurried around the front end and climbed into the passenger seat. They were off in an instant.

Chandler turned the truck right onto Chatam Avenue, as usual, but she didn't think a thing about it until he said, "I'll try to keep you from being late, but I promised I'd have money to someone early this morning."

"Late for what?"

"Work," he said, glancing at her in obvious confusion.

"But I don't have to go in to work today," Bethany pointed out, blinking.

The truck actually took a jerk sideways as he gaped at her. "You're not working today?"

"It's Friday."

He slapped a hand to his forehead. "Of all the insane… Tell me I didn't drag you out without any breakfast!"

She grimaced apologetically. "I only got up a few minutes before I heard you go out."

"Blast!" He whipped over to the side of the street and braked to a stop. "I'll take you back."

Torn between amusement and disappointment, she put on a smile and banished the other. At least he hadn't left without saying goodbye.

"No, it's okay. I'll eat later. I'm not even hungry yet. Go on. Keep your appointment."

"You're a sweetheart," he declared. Checking his mirrors, he started the truck moving again. "I'd take you back anyway, but Dovey was good enough to stable my horses at a very reasonable fee after Kreger sold the ranch out from under me, so I owe her. Her operation is always teetering on the edge of bankruptcy, though, and she called this morning to ask if I could pay early because she had a load of feed on its way. I just hopped out of bed and headed out. Then, I thought, oh, no, Bethany's got to get to work, so I ran back upstairs again."

"Sounds like Dovey woke you from a sound sleep."

"She did."

"She must need all the help she can get, then."

"She does," he admitted, "but I'm sorry about dragging you out like this. Guess my brain's not working yet."

"Aw, don't worry about it," Bethany told him, adding sheepishly, "I thought you were heading off to the rodeo without saying goodbye."

He slapped himself in the forehead again.

"I forgot! It's Friday!" Shaking his head, he huffed a disgusted breath. "Doesn't matter. I don't have to be there until three, and it's only a couple hours away. It'll be fine. In fact, tell you what, for being such a good sport about this, we'll stop off for breakfast somewhere on the way back from Dovey's. How does that work for you?"

"It works just fine," she said, smiling and settling in for the drive.

"I've done some stupid things," he said after a moment, "but this is one for the books." He started to chuckle, and soon they were both laughing.

She quite liked a man who could laugh at himself, Bethany decided. This one she could very easily love. In fact, she suspected that she already did.

It was a short trip. They exited the highway after only a couple miles and traveled on the feeder road for some distance before turning to the right. Skirting a cookie-cutter-type neighborhood, they drove down a narrow lane. The pavement ended abruptly after perhaps half a mile, but Chandler never slowed. The truck barreled along, throwing up dust behind it, until even that dirt track ended at a barbed-wire fence. A hard left took them through a narrow, overgrown drive and into a yard of crinkly, sunburned grass.

As before, when they'd come out here to get the horses in the earliest hours of the morning on the day of their wedding—had it really been a mere week?—Chandler drove right past the modest frame house. Beyond it, cobbled together from a variety of materials, lay a maze of corrals, several small outbuildings and a pair of sizable barns. He brought the truck to a stop in a wide, dusty circle at the end of the drive and got out.

A thin, older woman in blue jeans and boots emerged from one of the outbuildings and lifted a hand in greeting. She started toward them, flanked by a pack of mutts ranging in size from knee-high to big-enough-to-saddle. One of them, a black, longhaired dog with a curled tail and a missing ear, loped ahead to yelp a greeting. As the welcoming party drew near, Bethany saw that one of the dogs was blind and another was horribly scarred.

Curious, Bethany got out of the truck. She'd always wanted a dog, but her stepfather and Jay both had refused to have one.

"Hey, y'all," the woman greeted them.

"Hey, yourself," Chandler said. Striding forward, he removed a wad of folded bills from his shirt pocket and offered it to her. "Here you go."

The woman smiled. Fiftyish and whipcord lean, she had a leathery look about her, aided in part by hair the color of tanned hides, which she had tied back with a dark ribbon. She took the cash from Chandler's hand, saying, "Thanks. This'll help."

"So will the sacks of feed I've got in the back," Chandler said, jerking a thumb toward the truck. He glanced that way and saw that Bethany had gotten out of the cab.

The woman tried to disguise her curiosity with a friendly smile, but Bethany felt it nonetheless.

Chandler waved her over and made the introduction. "This is Dovey Crawlick. My wife, Bethany."

The older woman goggled. "Wife!"

Chuckling, Chandler said, "The one and only."

"I had no... When did... Glory be!" She leaned forward with an outstretched hand. "How do you do? Pleased to meet you."

"Fine. Thank you," Bethany replied, trying not to wince at the firm grasp.

Dovey lifted an eyebrow at Chandler, but he just rocked back on his heels, shrugging.

"You've been a busy boy," she said cheekily.

"Yes, ma'am." He lifted one foot and then another, pretending to examine them. "No moss on the soles of these boots."

He was enjoying this, Bethany realized, more pleased than she probably ought to be. Not wanting to betray herself, she went down on her haunches to pet the curly tailed dog. Chandler informed her that Dovey worked for a local vet, which abetted her inclination to rescue unwanted animals.

"Horses mostly," Dovey told her, waving toward the barns. "Costs a pretty penny, let me tell you." She looked around sharply and said, "There's the truck now."

"We'll let you get on about your business, then," Chandler said. "I need to feed my stock anyway. We're heading out to work in a couple hours."

"Good luck to you, then," Dovey said.

Chandler shook his head and pointed skyward. "It's all skill and the Man Upstairs."

Smiling, Dovey strode off toward the truck now idling in her yard. The dogs followed.

Chandler slid a hand beneath Bethany's arm, helping her to her feet. She wiped her hands on her leggings.

"Do you mind if I take time to feed my horses? I can take you home first if you want."

Bethany shook her head. "No, I don't mind."

Chandler smiled. "I appreciate that. Thanks."

"No problem." Actually, she was glad for the chance to spend more time with him.

They climbed back into the truck cab, and he drove it around to the nearest of the barns. After backing the vehicle inside, he went into a small room in the front corner and came out with a wheelbarrow. The rest of the barn was filled with two rows of stalls built of narrowly spaced metal pipes, one down each side of the building. Bethany got out and watched as Chandler heaved bags of feed from the bed of the truck and stacked them in the wheelbarrow. He pushed these into the small room and unloaded them, then returned for more. The final bag he wheeled down the center of the aisle to the very back of the barn, Bethany following on his heels.

No wonder those shoulders are so wide, she thought.

He finally stopped near the sliding gate of the final stall. Arroyo was a stocky, light brown horse with a smoky gray mane and tail, his broad back neatly bisected by a line of the same color. A lineback dun, Chandler had called him. He was the horse that Chandler used for steer wrestling.

Ginger Boy and Red Rover were a pair of matched bays with white blazes, reddish coats and black manes and tails. Each of them had bands of white, or stockings, on the lower front legs, and both were geldings. They were trained for team roping, and Chandler traded them off, using first one and then the other during competition.

The fourth animal, a beautiful black with black eyes, was a stallion. "His name is El Rey Ébano," Chandler told her. "It's Spanish for King Ebony. I call him Ébano for short." The horse tossed his head as if fully aware that they were talking about him. "He's full of himself, this fellow, but he has reason to be." He was no more proud of himself than Chandler was proud of him, though. That was obvious.

Bethany stood back while Chandler went about feeding and watering the animals. It was done within minutes, then he pushed the empty wheelbarrow back down the aisle. Bethany followed him, right into the little room. It was black as night in there and smelled of hay and oats. She looked around curiously, making out stacked bags of feed on a hay-covered floor, various cans and brooms and a pair of wide shovels as well as bales of something labeled "bedding." She assumed that was the shredded, spongy stuff on the stall floors. Chandler tilted the wheelbarrow up against one wall, turned and nearly mowed her down.

"Oops!" His big hands steadied her, grasping her by the upper arms.

She attempted to step back. But he didn't let her go.

She looked up, and for a long moment, they stood frozen. Bethany found that she couldn't quite breathe. His eyes gleamed in the darkness, and his head seemed to dip toward hers. She shifted her weight onto her toes, her heart slamming inside her chest. But then his hands dropped from her arms and she realized that she was staring at his cleft chin.

Clearing her throat, Bethany quickly turned away, embarrassed, and hurried to the truck. Chandler followed more slowly, and a few minutes later, the truck turned onto the dirt road. By the time they hit the pavement, Bethany's heartbeat had at last returned to normal. She hoped he hadn't noticed that she'd practically thrown herself at him back there.

They were almost to the highway when Chandler shifted in his seat and, without looking at her, said, "Thanks for your patience, especially after I hauled you out on your day off."

"I enjoyed it," Bethany said, and she had, very much. She'd have enjoyed it more if he'd actually kissed her. *Don't think about it,* she told herself. "I, ah, I've always liked animals."

He finally glanced her way. "Yeah? Me, too. Especially horses. I guess that's what drew me to Kreger to begin with. He lived on his grandparents' ranch and grew up around horses."

"The ranch you thought you'd invested in."

"The same."

"I'm sorry about how that turned out," she told him.

"Thanks. I'm trying to let that go, but it's not easy. Asher— that's my cousin, the lawyer—says I have no case because I had use of the property while I was giving Kreger money and no proof that it was anything but payment for use. The sale's final, so it's too late to file any sort of lien on the property anyway." He glanced at her as he guided the truck up the ramp onto the highway, saying, "Besides, what Kreger did to me is nothing compared to what that Jay character did to you. If you can survive that, I can survive this."

She propped her elbow on the edge of the door and laid her head on her upturned palm. "I thought he was saving me from the nightmare at home. And you know, I guess he did, even if it was all lies."

"I'd beg you to file charges on him, Bethany, if it wasn't for Matthew," Chandler told her.

She shook her head. "Like you, I have no proof."

"Even if you did," Chandler told her, "it would be too dangerous. He'd be acknowledged as Matthew's father, so he'd have rights there. I asked Ash about it."

She shuddered and said, "It's better this way. Matthew has the father he needs."

Chandler smiled at her. "I hope so. I'll do my best, God as my witness."

"Don't you think I know that?" she asked him softly. "Do you believe, for one minute, that I'd trust my son to you if I didn't know that you are the best dad I could ever give him?"

He nodded and looked away, and she had the distinct impression that he was blinking.

After a moment, he cleared his throat and asked, "Want to stop by the waffle place? Or did you have something else in mind?"

Bethany smiled. "The waffle place suits me just fine."

He suited her just fine. Even if he never came to love her, he would always be the husband of her heart.

He seemed to make an effort to dispel the awkwardness, so much so that they wound up chatting like old friends. All through breakfast, they talked. He told her about his older brothers. One, a banker in Dallas, had a wife, grown daughters and two grandchildren of his own, but the other had never married. They had a different mother than Chandler and Kaylie; she had died long ago, and Hubner had married a second time, only to be widowed again.

Bethany talked about her own father's death and how hard it had been for her mom. It had been harder still after she'd married Doyle Benjamin.

It was good, sitting there talking with him, but that moment back there in the barn hovered constantly in the back of Bethany's mind.

Had he really been tempted to kiss her? Or was her brain shrinking as her waistline expanded?

It had to be the latter.

She tried not to let that thought cast a pall on her enjoyment of the morning, and in truth, it did not, but when Chandler left for the rodeo a couple hours after taking her back to Chatam House, Bethany silently wished that she was going with him. Apparently, the idea never even occurred to Chandler, and she wasn't brave enough to suggest it, so if she was disappointed, well, she had no right to be.

But she was.

She definitely was.

Chapter Ten

Sighing, Bethany threw back the covers and sat up on the side of the bed. She'd called it a sleigh bed when she'd first seen it, but Magnolia had informed her that it was, "a French Empire burr chestnut with curved head- and footboards." Bethany had made the appropriately appreciative sounds, but in her opinion, its best attribute was the comfort of its mattress. Unfortunately, that comfy mattress made little difference tonight.

She knew that she would not be able to sleep until Chandler came home. It amazed her really. After Jay, she'd thought no man would ever be able to affect her again, but she was coming to realize that what she'd felt for Jay was a pale imitation of what she ought to have felt. In the end, all Jay had hurt was her pride. Chandler, she suspected, could break her heart without even knowing it.

Trying not to think about him, she'd kept herself busy by arranging the nursery and, this morning, attending church with the aunties. She'd happily gone to a Sunday school class for women her own age, where she'd sat with Cleo Ann, identified herself to the group at large as Bethany Chatam and explained that Chandler was competing in a rodeo in

Louisiana that weekend. She had put his name on the prayer list, and they had prayed for his safety and success.

Cleo Ann had asked how she and Chandler had gotten together, and Bethany had answered truthfully, saying that he'd picked her up on the side of the road after her car had broken down. Thankfully, no one had asked when that first meeting had occurred. The subject of the baby shower had come up, but Bethany had discouraged the idea because Chandler's aunts had already been so generous.

The rest of the day had passed quietly. Bethany had eaten lunch with Garrett and dinner with the aunties, spending the hours between by puttering around in the baby's room. She supposed that she was "nesting" because she couldn't stay out of there. She decided that she'd just look in there now, be sure that all was as she remembered.

Before she could stand, a cramp tightened her abdominal muscles. She let it run its course, breathing evenly until it waned. The pains had gradually returned after her visit to the emergency room, but she calmed her fear with prayer and knowledge. Remembering what the doctor had told her about Braxton-Hicks and all that she'd been able to glean about the condition via the Internet at work, she rose and pulled a big, misshapen T-shirt over the tank top that she wore with her usual loose-knit shorts.

Padding barefoot through the dark sitting room, she went straight to the nursery and turned on the colorful lamp that stood atop the highboy dresser. She wandered around, trailing her fingers across the furnishings, smiling at the color-blocked rug that softened the hardwood floor and matched the coverlet, which worked beautifully color-wise with the drapery. The bright yellow window coverings were somewhat more formal than Bethany would have chosen, but she wasn't about to complain, especially as they were permanent to the room.

Sweeping up a tiny stuffed horse with a pale blue saddle and soft yarn mane and tail, she sat down in the rocking chair that Chester had brought in from another room and pretended that she was cradling her son. Singing softly, she worked her way through every lullaby and baby song that she knew. She had just taken a breath when a sudden voice made her jump.

"What are you doing up at this hour?"

She looked around to find Chandler standing in the doorway, his boots in his hand. Her heart racing, she gasped, "You frightened me."

"Sorry." He set down the boots and walked across the floor in his stocking feet. "You didn't answer my question. Why aren't you asleep?"

She shrugged. "Just feeling kind of weird, I guess."

Frowning, he went down on his haunches beside her and lifted a hand to her forehead. "Maybe you're coming down with something."

"I'm fine." She smiled as she reached up to remove his hand from her brow. The baby suddenly moved. Bethany instinctively placed Chandler's hand on her abdomen, quipping, "I'm not the only one who can't sleep."

He stared at her belly as it rippled, little hillocks appearing here and there, only to smooth out again as the baby moved. Finally, Matthew subsided into stillness, and Chandler looked up at her with awe in his cinnamon eyes.

"Amazing," Chandler whispered.

Their gazes held for several long moments before he abruptly snatched his hand away and pushed up to his full height.

Bethany hurried to smooth over the sudden awkwardness, asking chattily, "So, how did it go this weekend?"

Chandler sent her a dark look and muttered, "Saw Kreger finally."

"Oh, dear."

"Would you believe that he actually wants to partner up again?"

Bethany sat up very straight. "You turned him down, of course. Didn't you?"

"Of course. He admitted to me that he sold the ranch because of gambling debts."

"Oh, Chandler, I'm so sorry."

He shook his head. "You know, it's probably for the best. I mean, it was wrong, but I sort of feel sorry for him."

"Why? He cheated you."

"Yeah, he did, but in the end, I came out of it better than he did. He says he's been living in his rig. His trailer's got one of those sleeping compartments in it. Thing's about the size of a coffin. I wouldn't want to try to sleep in there. Besides, if he hadn't done what he did, I wouldn't have met Drew. Might not have met you, either," he added softly. "I probably wouldn't even have been on that road then if Kreger had shown up at that rodeo." He waved a hand. "Anyway, the Bible says to forgive, and that's what I'm trying to do. Doesn't mean I want him hanging around, though."

He looked so dark that Bethany decided to change the subject. "Speaking of Drew and you, how did that go?"

Chandler brightened visibly. "We finished less than a tenth of a second out of first place."

"That's great!"

"It's in the money, anyway, but there's a lot more difference in first and second place than that fraction of a second."

"Financially, you mean."

He nodded. "And it doesn't help that I came in third in the tie-down and well out of it otherwise."

She sensed his frustration. "You'll find your stride," she told him encouragingly. "All you have to do is be patient."

"It's just that we're running out of time," Chandler groused.

"It's August already. We're having a baby in little more than two months, in case you've forgotten."

Bethany hauled her belly up out of the chair, quipping, "You're kidding me, right? You've seen what I'm lugging around here."

His mouth twitched. "You say that all the time."

"What?"

"You're kidding me."

She frowned in puzzlement. "No, I'm not. How could I? Just look at me." She pressed down the fabric of her T-shirt, emphasizing the size of her belly.

Chandler grinned. "You say, 'You're kidding me' all the time. It's like your trademark phrase. Whatever anyone says, you come back with 'You're kidding me' or 'No kidding' or something to that effect."

Bethany blinked. "I guess I do. I hadn't realized. Sorry."

He chuckled. "It's not a complaint. I think it's cute."

Cute? She wrinkled her nose. Cute wasn't exactly how she wanted Chandler to think of her. Then again, for a woman shaped like a beached whale, it could be worse. She stepped closer and reached up to smooth back the lock of hair that had fallen forward over his brow.

"I just don't want to irritate you, not when you work so hard all the time," she said softly.

His sudden frown made her wonder what she'd said wrong. "I'm not the only one who works."

"I sit in a chair, answer the phone and smile at people all day," she pointed out drily. "You *work*." She tilted her head, studying his handsome face. "In fact, you look tired. You should go to bed and get a good night's sleep."

"That makes two of us."

She smiled. "I will if you will." A sharp, sudden pain made her gasp and grab her side.

Chandler clasped her protectively, one hand going to the

small of her back and the other to her abdomen. "Is it a contraction?"

She shook her head, caught her breath and said, "Matthew just kicked me in the ribs."

Chandler breathed out a sigh. "So you haven't been having the cramps?"

She grimaced. "I have, but it's okay. I know what they are now, so it doesn't scare me so much anymore."

"So much?" he repeated, beetling his brow.

"I've learned to pray when I get frightened," she told him, patting his chest.

"Good idea," he said approvingly, covering her hand with his. "I find it helps me sleep sometimes, too."

Bethany smiled. "Yes, I've found that to be true. Maybe that's what we need right now."

Chandler pulled back slightly. "You mean that we should pray together?"

"Yes, please," she answered, closing her eyes before he could beg off.

After a long pause, Chandler began to softly speak. "We thank You, Lord, that little Matthew is so strong and active, and we trust You to keep him that way, but it understandably frightens his mom when those awful cramps come. Please spare her that pain and give us all peace and rest this night. Amen."

"Amen," she whispered. She looked up to find him smiling down at her. "Thank you for that," she said. He nodded. "Good night."

"Good night," he returned.

The kiss just seemed to happen, a natural consequence of all that had passed in the moments before she lifted her face and he lowered his head. The moment his lips met hers, she knew that this was what she wanted, needed from him, what she had been waiting for. She felt her hands slide around his neck, heard the soft sound that he made as he pulled her closer, his arms holding her tight. He was her husband, and she had never felt more like his wife than in this moment of sweet joining.

If only, she thought. *If only this was a true marriage.*

But how could she expect that of him? He didn't really want her any more than Jay had. How could he, fool that she was? Chandler had done his best to help her, but she and the baby were nothing more than burdens to him. All of which meant that this lovely kiss was a terrible mistake. Saddened, she made herself turn her head away.

He released her instantly, lurching back as if she'd thrown cold water on him. She quickly fled to the safety of her own bedroom. There she sat down on the side of the bed again, feeling foolish and scalded. After a time, she went to God, asking that He help her be satisfied with what He had given her—or help her make it all that she wanted it to be.

So much for keeping emotional distance, Chandler thought disgustedly. He'd managed for a time—if thinking about her every waking minute and missing her something awful when he was away could be termed "emotional distance." Still, he'd managed to keep from kissing her that day at Dovey's. Only to kiss her in their suite at Chatam House.

Mentally kicking himself all night long didn't do a bit of good. He couldn't take back that ill-advised kiss and he couldn't get it out of his mind. He dropped off, finally, thinking about it—and woke again on Monday morning with it playing vividly in his memory.

"Stupid, stupid, stupid," he chanted softly, dressing quickly in old jeans and a tan T-shirt.

He and Drew had agreed to practice three days a week, the same days that Bethany worked, Tuesday, Wednesday and Thursday. That left Monday and Friday for everything else, including traveling to and from weekend competition. The bigger rodeos ran two, even three weeks, but most were four or five days long. At this time of year, though, those venues were far from the hot South. He and Drew had reasons to stick closer to home, which meant that Chandler found himself with a rare day off, a day when he could have simply relaxed.

Chandler knew, however, that relaxation would be impossible this day. After pulling on his socks, he caught up his working boots and his sweat-stained straw hat and tiptoed out of the suite, thinking that Bethany would almost certainly still be asleep.

Pausing at the top of the stairs to pull on his boots, he balanced on first one foot and then another before trotting down in search of breakfast. His mood lightened considerably as he drew near the kitchen and caught the aroma of Hilda's cream biscuits. He could almost taste them. His stomach rumbling, he dropped his hat onto one of several pegs affixed to the wall before shoving through the swinging door. Hilda straightened and turned away from the big, old-fashioned stove, her rotund frame surprisingly agile. Beaming a welcome at him, she waved a large pan of golden-brown biscuits in one hand.

"Ah, he's up and about, is he? Well, come on and get your breakfast, then."

Inhaling appreciatively, he started to follow her to the small, sturdy, rectangular table situated before the brick fireplace, but then he halted. "Is that coffee I smell?"

The aunties were devoted to their tea. That being the case, Chandler had intended to pick up a can of coffee for himself, but he'd taken most of his breakfasts away from the house for one reason or another, so had never gotten around to stopping by the store.

Hilda nodded toward the table, saying, "You can thank your wife for that."

Surprised, Chandler leaned sideways a bit to look around Hilda, who was almost as wide as she was tall. Bethany sat at the table in baggy denim shorts and a blue sleeveless top, her face freshly scrubbed and heartbreakingly beautiful. As she tilted her pretty head, smiling shyly, her dark, sleek hair swung lushly about her slender shoulders. Chandler's breath caught in his throat.

"Good morning."

"Morning," he managed.

"You're too quick," Hilda told him, plunking the pan of biscuits onto a hot pad in the center of the table. "The missus here was going to bring you breakfast in bed."

Chandler froze, stunned to think of his pregnant wife serving him breakfast in bed. Hilda trundled off to take up a red enamel tray from the enormous metal worktable that took up a significant amount of floor space in the cavernous room. Carrying the tray to the table, she placed it in front of the chair across from Bethany's then forked up two tall, flaky biscuits.

"Tray was all ready," she said. "It was just waiting on this. You saved her the trip."

Hilda jerked her head, all but ordering Chandler to sit. He walked over and sat, deeply touched, and surveyed the contents of the tray: butter and Hilda's famous cinnamon fig preserves, cantaloupe and a cup of fragrant black coffee, plus those two high biscuits. His mouth watered.

"Y'all didn't have to go to so much trouble," he said, reaching for the butter knife.

"No trouble on my part," Hilda pointed out, waddling off toward the stove.

Chandler looked at Bethany. "Thank you, especially for the coffee. But you shouldn't be serving anyone breakfast in bed."

"The dumbwaiter comes up right outside our door,"

Bethany reminded him quietly, looking down at her own empty plate. She reached for a tall glass of milk beside it. "It's just that you looked so tired last night, and I..." She let the sentence dwindle away with a glance.

"She has an ulterior motive," Hilda announced loudly. "She wants to go with you today."

Chandler felt his eyebrows jump toward his hairline as Bethany tucked her chin, her cheeks pinkening. His pleasure at the request dismayed him. All the more reason, he told himself, to maintain some distance between the two of them. Pity he couldn't seem to do it. At least he managed to keep his tone level and noncommittal as he went about breaking open the hot biscuits. "That so? Not much of interest going on with me today. Thought I'd clean the horse stalls and trailer."

Bethany reached for the pan and transferred a biscuit to her own plate, keeping her gaze carefully averted. "I don't mind. I like it out at Dovey's place."

"Awful hot outside."

"I won't melt."

Chandler buttered his biscuits and slathered them with fig jelly, trying to marshal his defenses. "Wouldn't be much for you to do."

She looked up, hope softening her breathtaking blue eyes. "I can hold a water hose, you know."

Chandler tried to bolster his objections. "Horses can be dangerous. Given your condition, do you think it's wise to take such a chance?"

"Cindy's around horses all day every day," she argued gently.

He couldn't refute that. Besides, he had absolutely no defense against that pleading tone. He had no defenses against *her*. In truth, he didn't even know why he bothered resisting. She charmed him, had since he'd first laid eyes on her perched there on that stool in the diner. He gave up.

"Okay, come along, then."

Bethany beamed as brightly as if he'd given her a big, shiny diamond, which he'd have liked very much to do. Fat chance of that. Even if he could have afforded it, he doubted that Bethany would have taken it. She'd probably be happier with her freedom.

"I'll pack you a picnic lunch," Hilda announced, not even bothering to pretend that she hadn't been eavesdropping.

"That's wonderful!" Bethany exclaimed, spreading her smile around the room, from Chandler to Hilda and back again. "Thank you."

Still beaming, she smeared jam on half a biscuit and stuffed it into her mouth. Chandler shook his head. Who'd have thought watching a woman smile and eat a biscuit could be so fascinating?

He downed his own biscuits in two bites each, then reached for three more. Bethany finished a second biscuit and started to rise, saying she would help Hilda make their lunch, at which point Hilda pointed a butcher knife at her and ordered, "Sit yourself down and finish your milk and fruit, missy. You're growing a babe there."

"Yes, ma'am." Obviously tickled, Bethany shared a smile with Chandler and dutifully gobbled up her melon before gulping down her milk. Finished, she dabbed daintily at the corners of her mouth with her napkin and sedately rose.

She looked ridiculously gorgeous in her ragged, knee-length denim shorts, form-fitting blue sleeveless top and tall red boots. Chandler remembered the way the baby had moved beneath his hand last night, and it was all he could do not to pull Bethany onto his lap and cradle them both. He knew that it was insane to take her with him. Keeping his distance would most assuredly be the safer, wiser course, but it was beyond him to deny her this or anything else she seemed to want. If only she wanted him.

Oh, Lord, help me, he prayed silently as he finished his breakfast and she went to help Hilda put up their lunch. *I'm finding that my father was right all along. I'm not a very wise man.*

Worse, he wasn't even sure that he wanted the wisdom that he so obviously lacked, for he had the sad suspicion that it would come at the price of a shattered heart.

"Can I ask you something?" Bethany said, sitting sideways on a saddle atop a low rack in the back of his pickup truck.

Chandler smiled to himself. She'd been asking questions all morning, while he forked out and swept the stalls, spread new bedding and fed, watered and groomed the horses. She'd helped in small ways, passing him pitchfork or broom, brushes or combs, pulling bedding from the bales. He'd made sure that he kept himself between her and the horses, but she couldn't resist reaching around him to dispense pats and rubs. Neither he nor the horses minded a bit.

He'd asked her if she'd ever thought about riding, and she'd replied that she'd always wanted to learn but had never had the chance. He'd blurted that he would teach her after the baby came, and she'd clapped her hands in glee. Praying that he'd have the chance to follow through, he spread an old blanket over the tailgate and bed of his truck, which he'd backed into the barn earlier.

His stomach growled like a surly wolf. Perching on the edge of the tailgate, he twisted around to reach into the cooler that Hilda had packed for them. After rummaging about for a moment, he came up with an apple and a bottle of water.

"Ask away," he said, biting into the apple.

"Don't you ever worry about getting hurt?"

He lowered the apple, the bottle of water in his other fist. "No, not really."

"Not even when you're leaping off a horse to grab a full-grown steer by the horns?"

"I don't *leap*," he said with a chuckle. "It's sort of a slide out of the saddle."

"Leap, slide, whatever. It's a full-grown animal and it has horns!"

He pushed back his hat with the cap end of the water bottle, touched that she seemed concerned for him. "Look, everyone gets hurt at some point. That's rodeo. That's sport in general. I couldn't compete at all if I wasn't willing to risk injury. That said, I do everything I can to protect myself, which is why I practice all the time, why I keep my gear in tip-top shape, why I concentrate and constantly work on my technique." He tapped the bottle against his knee and told her what he hadn't told anyone else, "That's why the last thing I do before I enter the arena is pray."

"I wouldn't have pegged you as a praying man when we first met," she commented gently.

He sighed. "Yeah, I know. But it's always been the case. I—I guess I just thought I couldn't show my faith, that it made me…I don't know, less tough, maybe." He shook his head at his own stupidity. "And to be perfectly honest, I guess it has to do with my dad, too. You know, that PK thing."

"PK?"

"Preacher's kid."

"Ah. Yes, I can see that. I actually think that's part of the problem on your dad's end, too. He's a minister, so his kid should do more noble things than everyone else's."

Chandler sent her a surprised look. "You figured that out, did you?"

She shrugged and said, "Frankly, I think he's a little hurt that none of his children followed him into the ministry."

mean, he says and, I'm sure, believes that everyone has to be true to his or her own calling, but it would be a natural thing to secretly hope that someone would take up the mantle, so to speak."

Suddenly Chandler remembered talking with Drew about their sons one day roping together. He'd thought then how cool it would be if his son should follow in his footsteps. Why hadn't he realized that his own father might feel the same?

"Oh, wow," Chandler said. "I never thought of that. And he never said anything."

"He wouldn't," Bethany remarked. "He'd see it as putting himself in God's place. He always says everyone is called to something, but that we must be sure it's God's voice we hear and not our own or someone else's."

Chandler nodded at that. He'd heard the same all his life, and he'd always firmly believed that he was meant to rodeo, at least for now. Later, he hoped to be able to concentrate on raising and training horses. He'd tried to explain that to his father, but Hub hadn't understood.

"You're talking about occupation," he would say. "I'm talking about ministry. What is your *ministry?*"

Now, suddenly, Chandler wondered the same thing himself. If God meant him to compete in rodeo, and Chandler believed that He did, then what was the purpose? Where was his ministry in that?

He thought of Drew's openness about his own faith, and it hit Chandler that for years now his focus had been on winning and, if he were honest, rubbing his father's nose in it, not in living for God. Had he been half as out there as Drew, no telling who he might have encouraged or influenced. He might even have made a difference in Pat Kreger's life.

Sharply stung, Chandler bowed his head right then and there, without so much as a word of explanation to Bethany, and silently told God how sorry he was and how wrong he'd been.

"I want to be the man that You would have me be, Lord. I want to be the husband, the father, the son, the brother, even the cowboy that You would have me be. So no more ignoring Your plans in favor of my own, no more living for that next win. Now I just want to live for You."

That, he suddenly realized, meant doing something he had thus far avoided. He had admit to his father what had happened with Kreger and apologize for all those times he'd refused to listen. Only then could he really start getting right with God.

He looked up to find Bethany kneeling in front of him, concern drawing a line between her eyes.

"You okay?" she asked gently.

He cleared his throat. "Getting there."

She tilted her head as if thinking that through. He smiled, feeling lighter, brighter, and lifted the half-eaten apple.

"Aren't you hungry?"

She sat back on her heels. "I am, actually."

"Let's dig in."

She shifted around and reached into the cooler, coming up with chicken salad sandwiches, hardboiled eggs and crunchy slices of peppered cucumber, along with a wealth of tasty accompaniments. They feasted, rhapsodizing about the food.

It seemed to Chandler as if they were pretending to be what they wanted the world to think them to be, the average married couple, and he wondered what might have happened if they'd met the way people normally met. Would they have fallen in love and married? He doubted that he'd have done more than look her over, think her extremely attractive and turn away, intent on the next contest, never knowing what he'd lost. He was glad, heartbreakingly glad, that he hadn't missed knowing her, even if it was bound to end for him in disappointment and pain. Not that he had any right to ask more of her.

The woman was giving him a son, for pity's sake, literally *giving* him a son! He felt like an ungrateful fool for wanting more from her.

But he did.

Oh, he did.

Even so, he would humbly accept God's will for his life, whatever it might be. That lesson, at least, he had finally learned.

Chapter Eleven

The newlyweds returned to the house late Monday afternoon filthy and exhausted. Magnolia regretted calling them into the parlor, but like her sisters, she had been eager to know if their outing together had gone well. Unfortunately it was impossible to tell under all that grime.

"Would you like tea, dears?" she asked, waving a hand at the tray on the table.

"Uh, no," Chandler replied, wiping perspiration from his brow with the back of his hand. He glanced at Bethany, adding, "not for me, anyway."

The sisters were under no illusions about this marriage. They didn't know the details of Chandler and Bethany's relationship, but not even Odelia bought the notion that Chandler had actually fathered Bethany's baby. The aunts knew their nephew better than that and couldn't understand how his own father did not. She supposed it had to do with the dynamics of the parent-and-child relationship. Whatever the truth of Chandler and Bethany's situation, it was clear to all three of his aunts that Chandler had married Bethany for other reasons, reasons that had to do with that oily attorney Haddon.

Odelia insisted that Chandler had somehow rescued

Bethany from "a fate worse than death." Magnolia scoffed, but secretly she wasn't sure that Odelia was entirely wrong.

Regardless of the reasons for the marriage, however, it was evident to all of them that things were not quite as they should be between the young couple. Carol had reported that they slept in separate bedrooms, and neither seemed particularly overjoyed with their situation. It was good to see them spending time together, though, even if the results were rather, well, fragrant. In fact, if she was not mistaken, Odelia was pinching her nose behind her hanky.

"No tea for me, either," Bethany said, holding out her hands to display streaks of dirt on her forearms. "All I want is a shower."

"Obi-usly, ewe two hab been busy," Odelia said from behind her hanky.

"You noticed," Chandler quipped. "We were cleaning the horse trailer. It was dirtier than I thought. Boots are clean, anyway. We hit them with the water hose. Otherwise, I think I have more stable than skin on me right now. So, see you later, if that's okay."

"Go, go," Hypatia said with a chuckle.

They went out into the foyer and up the stairs, taking their odor with them.

Odelia lowered her handkerchief, the tip of her nose bright pink in contrast to the bright orange pantsuit that she wore, complete with earrings of fake, orange-slice candies. "I thought they went on a picnic," she said petulantly.

"Hilda only said that she'd packed them a picnic lunch," Magnolia pointed out.

"Well, picnic or cleaning a horse trailer, whatever they were doing, they were doing it together," Hypatia said.

Odelia brightened. "That's true."

"It doesn't mean that we don't still have praying to do," Magnolia warned.

Hypatia sighed. "I fear you're right. The marriage may have come before the romance in this case."

"Let's hope the baby doesn't, too," Odelia muttered.

Magnolia gasped. It was the most perceptive thing she'd heard her sister say yet.

"Thanks for taking me with you today," Bethany said. The day had been joy and agony for her, joy because they had worked together like a team and agony because she wanted so much more with him, so much that she feared she would never have.

"Thanks for the help," he returned. He climbed the stairs a step behind her, as if to catch her should she fall. Of course, that could be wishful thinking on her part. He might just be too tired to keep up. The man had worked like a Trojan today.

"I didn't do much."

"You did enough."

She smiled. "It was fun."

"Well, if that's your idea of fun," he drawled, "I'd hate to see your idea of hard work."

She laughed. He was the one who had worked hard, and she believed wholeheartedly that he'd enjoyed every minute of it.

Something, however, had changed after their conversation about his dad. She wasn't sure what, really, but she knew that Chandler seemed both more relaxed and more pensive afterward. He'd scrubbed the horse trailer with silent doggedness, yet she'd sensed that he was somewhat distracted.

Once in the suite they went their separate ways.

Bethany took a long, hot shower, dried her hair and managed a little nap before dinner. Chandler came to the table freshly scrubbed but very quiet. Even the aunties noticed.

"Chandler, dear," Hypatia asked at one point, "are you well?"

"Getting there," he replied with an absent smile.

It was the same answer that he'd given Bethany earlier in the day, and she could only wonder what exactly that meant. He disappeared into his room as soon as they returned to the suite after dinner, and she didn't see him again until the morning. Even then he seemed preoccupied, so she was surprised when, instead of dropping her off, he parked the truck and got out to walk up to the door of the Single Parent Ministry building with her.

It didn't end there, though. Not only did he open the door for her, he followed her inside. Glancing back warily, she carried her handbag to the reception desk and dropped it into a drawer. Chandler, meanwhile, stood watching...and waiting, it seemed.

Calling out a cheery "Good morning!" Hub appeared from the hallway. He froze when he saw Chandler there.

"Dad," Chandler said, shifting around to face the older man. "Got a minute? I need to talk to you."

Hubner looked to Bethany, who knew no more than he did. Concerned, she started forward, ready to intervene if necessary. Chandler sent her a taut smile.

"It's okay, hon. No fireworks today, I promise. I just need a word in private with my dad."

Hubner opened his mouth as if to speak, but then he simply nodded, turned and walked back toward his office. Bethany rushed to Chandler.

"What's going on?"

He reached toward her, his hand landing in the vicinity of her waist. "It's time," he said. "Don't worry. I prayed about this for hours last night."

"You're going to tell him about us," she surmised softly.

He shook his head. "No. I wouldn't do that to you and

Matthew. What's between us stays between us. This is about me and him."

She flashed back to the day before and their conversation in the back of the truck. Something warm and bright trickled through her. She wasn't sure why, but she knew that this was a special moment. As if to reinforce that feeling, Chandler leaned in and kissed her cheek before following his father into the hallway.

Bethany went back to her desk, sat down and bowed her head, praying that this might be the first step in a meeting of the hearts between father and son.

Oddly, he'd expected to feel like a child again about to face his father's disappointment and correction. Instead, Chandler felt strong and sure, even at peace, though he had not yet done what he'd come here to do. Hubner stood beside the door. Chandler stepped past him into the cramped office and glanced about as his father closed the door and moved around to sit behind his desk.

The room felt familiar, though Chandler had never been in here before. He recognized the carved cross hanging on one wall and the framed verse on a small easel on one of the bookshelves behind the desk. It was John 6:5-6.

Then Jesus lifted up His eyes, and seeing a great multitude coming toward Him, He said to Philip, "Where shall we buy bread, that these may eat?" But this He said to test him, for He Himself knew what He would do.

Smiling to himself, Chandler bowed his head. The aunties were right. God undoubtedly knew exactly what He was doing and why.

"I'm sorry, Dad," he said, unable to leave it for another

moment. "You were right all along. I let Kreger drag me through dive after dive, and in the end, he cheated and ran out on me."

The chair creaked as Hubner sat forward. Glancing at his father's shocked face, Chandler stepped up and dropped down onto one of a pair of padded wooden chairs arranged in front of the desk.

"Don't misunderstand me," he rushed to say, folding his forearms against the desktop, "I believe—I *know*—that I'm called to rodeo. It's what I'm meant to do. But I'm also meant to use that as a way to witness, if only by proclaiming myself a Christian and living like it. I didn't get that until Kreger flaked out on me. Actually, I didn't get it until Bethany..." He shook his head. That was beside the point. "What I'm saying is, I'm sorry I didn't listen to you."

Hubner sat back again, lacing his fingers over his rounded belly. "Cheated and ran out, you say?"

"Yes, sir." Chandler briefly explained, ending with, "It's okay, though. I have a new partner now, and things are starting to happen for us. I just want you to know, it's not all about winning for me now. It's about being the man I'm supposed to be, the man God wants me to be."

His father stared at him for a long time, then he gripped the arms of his chair and sat up straight. "I don't know what to say, son. I truly did not want this disappointment for you, but I can't pretend I'm surprised or heartbroken. Frankly, I expect it's for the best. I always felt that Kreger pulled you away from us, away from your real purpose in life. Frankly, I thought that you were the one most likely to...rather, the one best suited for..." He grimaced, and Chandler smiled with wry understanding.

Pretty smart, that little wife of his.

"Dad, I'm not cut out for the pulpit. You know that."

Hubner steepled his hands. "I know it *now*. I admit that it took me a while to see it." He rubbed a hand over his face, sighing. "Took me a long time to see it. Hard to see what you don't want to."

"Amen," Chandler said to that. Then he caught sight of the decorative clock in the shape of a church on the corner of his father's desk and rose to his feet. "I've got to be going. Drew's expecting me in Stephenville. I just wanted...I just wanted to apologize."

He turned and moved swiftly toward the door, only to draw up short when his father spoke his name.

"Chandler."

His hand hovered over the doorknob. "Yes, sir?"

"Thank you."

Chandler nodded and went out, leaving his father with his head bowed in deep contemplation.

Neither father nor son offered any description of what had passed between them, and Bethany dared not ask. Hubner seemed as preoccupied as his son had the day before. Conversely, Chandler was in an expansive mood when he picked her up from work that afternoon. He chatted animatedly about the day's practice as they drove around town on errands, picking up his dry cleaning, gassing the truck, purchasing shaving cream and razor blades. They didn't get back to the house until dinnertime.

After the meal, they wound up in the sitting room of their suite, side by side on the sofa, watching TV on the screen mounted above the fireplace mantel. Happily, they liked the same program. When it was over, Chandler switched off the set.

"This is better than what we had out at the ranch," Chandler told her, aiming the remote at the screen. "I've gotta give it to the old dears, they may live in a hundred-and-fifty-year-old house, surrounded by antiques, but they do try to keep up."

Bethany chuckled and bumped her shoulder against his. "Do you know, I found Odelia on the computer in the study not long ago, surfing the Internet in search of jewelry."

He laughed. "Is that where she finds her earrings?"

Bethany giggled. "I thought there was a crazy earring store around here somewhere."

He laughed even harder at that, until Bethany playfully scolded him. "We shouldn't make fun of her. She's such a darling."

"Oh, she is," he agreed. "They all are. I wouldn't change a hair on any of their heads. Or yours for that matter." His expression suddenly grew serious, and he skimmed a hair over her head. "You have beautiful hair."

"Thank you."

"And beautiful eyes."

"Thank you again."

"Beautiful everything."

She dropped her gaze, pleased and a little embarrassed. "I'm glad you think so."

"Sweetheart, I don't think it, I know it. It can't help but improve a man when he's got a woman like you on his arm."

"I don't think you need improving," she told him shyly.

"Yeah, I do," he said. "More than you know and in ways you can't see."

"What do you mean?" she asked, surprised he could think that about himself. As far as she could tell, he was the next thing to perfect.

He swallowed and shook his head, saying, "I think I better go now." He got up and headed for his bedroom, wishing her a good night.

Sighing, Bethany went to her own room, but she hadn't given up. She wanted this marriage, and she wanted this man. If only she could make him want her, too.

* * *

Watching TV, Chandler decided, could be a dangerous thing with a wife like his. She had no notion how tempting she was, and because he knew his limits, he'd figured that he better find something else to do tonight.

He flexed his hands inside the new gloves, feeling the lanoline with which he'd treated the leather ooze a bit. He was working them on an old rope so the emollient wouldn't destroy the stiffness of a new one. A limp rope wasn't good for anything more than tying bundles and tricks. He made a loop and tossed it at one of the standing plant holders scattered among the tables arranged around the softly chuckling fountain.

"You better not let Magnolia catch you roping her beautiful plants."

He smiled in the direction of his wife's amused voice, blinded by the light from a bulb mounted above the sunroom door. "Why do you think I missed?"

She laughed softly. What a beautiful sound it was, healing, almost, in its purity.

"Mind if I watch?"

He shrugged. "Nothing much to see."

"I think there is," she said, taking a seat on one of the chaises beside the fountain. "I find all these little jobs and the many tools of your trade fascinating."

"Yeah? Me, too," Chandler confessed. "Rodeo's pretty high-tech these days, but there's something comforting and powerful about doing things you know countless others have done before you, things that only a select few really appreciate now."

"I can understand that. When you get down to it, I suppose having a baby is the same way."

"I suppose it is at that," he said, pausing to think about it.

"One more thing we have in common," she said.

"What do you mean?"

"Well, we've both been betrayed by people we trust. We've both lost parents. We both love our remaining family. And we've both led fairly unconventional lives. Just look at what you do for a living. You make your own way. None of that nine-to-five stuff for you. I admire that. Wish my own lack of convention was as admirable. I mean, my so-called marriage to Jay was anything but normal."

"And look at us now," Chandler said, wincing at the edge of discontent in his own voice. "Ours isn't exactly a conventional marriage, either, Bethany," he couldn't help adding.

"No, it's not," she said, "but maybe we're not cut out for conventional."

"Maybe we're not," he agreed. "So, okay, my unconventional wife, let's rope us some chairs. Mags won't cut up at that. What do you say?"

Bethany laughed. "Rope all the chairs you want, cowboy. I'll even sit in them if you like."

"That won't be necessary," he told her. In truth, if he ever got a loop on her, he wasn't entirely sure he could let her go again.

It was nearly eleven when they finally turned in that night, but sleep eluded Bethany for hours afterward. She couldn't stop going over every moment that they had spent together lately. Funny how a few happy days could color a girl's world, she mused.

Cleaning stalls and eating a picnic lunch in the back of a truck hadn't been a romantic interlude by any means, and yet she had come away feeling as if she was a part of something real, one of a pair, half of a couple. The ensuing days had only reinforced that notion. The truth, of course, was that they were friends who happened to be legally wed, nothing more, and that only because Chandler was such a good man.

He had done so much for her. She wished that she could do something good for him in return. If only she could find a way to fully reconcile Chandler with his father. She felt they'd made a step in that direction, but it seemed a wary step at best. They were both such wonderful men, and each had been so very kind to her, despite the difficulties that she had added to their relationship, but they continued to circle each other like wary beasts, neither looking for a fight but neither coming closer. Lately she had been tempted to tell Hub the truth about her and Chandler so he would know what a truly fine man this son of his was, but she hadn't for two reasons.

One was entirely selfish. She wanted Chandler to be the father of this child and her husband for real, not just in the eyes of the world and his family. The second reason was simply that Chandler *was* her husband, at least in name, and she wouldn't go against his express wishes. Hub was *his* father. Marrying her had been *his* decision, his plan. In this case it was *his* truth to tell. Or not.

Chandler was set to leave Thursday morning for a rodeo in New Mexico. Why that should have Bethany feeling slightly panicked, she didn't know, but no sooner did her eyes open that morning than she threw on a robe and went to his room. Standing there in the doorway, she could feel her heart beating against her breastbone like a caged bird fluttering its wings.

"How long will you be gone?" she asked, trying to keep the tremor from her voice.

Chandler stuffed socks into his rolling duffel bag and looked up. "Probably be the wee hours of Monday morning before I get in."

Bethany nodded.

"I'll be done here in a minute, then I'll take you to work,"

Chandler went on. "Kaylie's going to give you a ride home this afternoon."

She managed a smile to let him know that she was appreciative, and then she took her courage in both hands and wrung it until the words she wanted came out. "If you could wait until then, I could go with you."

He froze in the act of zipping the bag.

"O-or I could ask Hub for the day off," she plunged on desperately.

Chandler slowly finished zipping the bag and straightened, turning slightly to face her. Her hopes plummeted. So sure was she that he was going to shoot her down, she began throwing up barriers herself.

"Oh, but…I—I do have a doctor's appointment on Monday afternoon, a-and I'm coming up on seven months, which means I won't be able to travel soon anyway, so…"

"So if you're going to go, it had better be now," Chandler said. He pursed his lips, looking thoughtful, and added, "I expect I could get you back in time for your appointment, and Kaylie will probably fill in for you today. I'll call her while you go pack." With that, he reached for his cell phone in his hip pocket.

Elated, Bethany was too stunned for a moment to do anything more than gape, but then Chandler made a shooing motion with one hand and began dialing his phone with the thumb of the other. Holding her belly with both hands, Bethany spun and ran back to her room, where she quickly threw things into her battered old suitcase. Her heart was beating double-time now, but for an entirely different reason. She was going with Chandler. They would be together for the whole, long weekend.

"Thank You," she whispered at the ceiling. "Thank You, thank You, thank You."

* * *

They drove away from Buffalo Creek Thursday at noon, heading for Lovington, New Mexico. It was a seven-hour trip that turned into nearly nine. Chandler didn't mind. Despite having to stop every hour so Bethany could make a dash for the ladies' room, he was thankful for the opportunity to get to know her better.

She finally told him all about Jay Carter, how he'd approached her at a football game during her senior year in high school. She'd known he was older, but she'd been flattered by the attention. He'd told her later that he didn't know why he'd stopped there that night, that it must have been fate. He'd claimed to have broken up with a long-term girlfriend and to be at loose ends. Chandler figured the creep had been trolling for a sweet young thing he could con. He'd hit the jackpot in Bethany. The brutality and hopelessness of her home life coupled with her youth had made her ripe pickings.

Carter, or Widener, had courted her assiduously but quietly over the next several months, aided by the travel supposedly required for his job. On the day of her high school graduation, they had eloped. The marriage, of course, had not been legal because the license had never been filed.

Chandler couldn't help being glad about that. If he could have, he'd have spared her the pain and trauma that Carter had perpetrated, but they might not have married otherwise. No matter how it turned out in the end, he was glad to be a part of her life now.

She was a good sport, fine company, a quick wit and a giggle box, seemingly ready to laugh at everything, even after all she'd been through. She was keen to learn all that he could tell her about rodeo. He hadn't talked so much in…well, he didn't think he'd ever talked so much. He hadn't realized just how much he knew about rodeo, either. She hadn't realized how complicated the business end of it all was.

"You need an accounting degree to figure it all out!"

"Or a lot of experience."

"Or a manager!"

"There are some. Right now, Cindy's kind of doing that for the team, and I'm piggybacking on her efforts for my individual events."

"Do a lot of wives do that?" Bethany asked.

"I imagine so."

He waited for her to say that someday maybe she could do it, but she just bit her lip and finally lapsed into silence. It didn't last. After a while she sent him a considering look and remarked, "I noticed that you have several saddles, more saddles than horses. Why so many?"

He chuckled and answered, "Different saddles for different purposes. Won some of them."

That sent them off into a discussion of prizes, which wound up with him promising to dig out some of his buckles, spurs and other whatnots. Most of it was pretty minor, but some of it was excellent stuff. Most of it was packed into the boxes in the attic.

"You need a display case," she decided, "a big one."

Shaking his head, he said, "I need to win some real money." Rolling his eyes upward, he added softly, "Please, God." If he could start winning regularly, then he might have something to offer her, something more than a last name for her son, some reason for her to consider making this marriage real.

Chapter Twelve

He won nearly seventeen thousand dollars, coming in first in all three of his events. Seven thousand was his share of the team roping winnings, and for the first time in his career, Chandler picked up a sponsor. That meant that a portion of his entry fees would be covered for the next four months, until the national finals in mid-December.

Bethany actually hugged the half-dozen dark blue, long-sleeved shirts with the sponsor's logo on the sleeves before carefully packing them into his kit. Just seeing that was worth more to Chandler than the financial reward. He liked the feeling that she might be proud of him, liked it very much. It gave him hope.

They were both giddy with triumph, and let Drew and Cindy talk them into a celebratory dinner. The two couples had prayed together every evening before he and Drew went about their business. They had also attended worship services at the arena that Sunday morning before the last performance and were well on their way to becoming fast friends. After the leisurely meal, however, it became obvious to Chandler that Bethany was too tired to make the drive back to Buffalo Creek, so they waved goodbye to the Shaws and stayed one more night in Lovington.

They'd given up their room that morning, so they had to switch motels. That was no problem, even in a town of only 9,500 permanent residents. Until they ran into an unexpected fellow guest.

Chandler was lifting the bags out of the backseat of the cab while Bethany waited at the front of the truck when a car playing loud music pulled up and a door opened. Chandler groaned inwardly when Patrick Kreger practically fell out onto the pavement. Laughing uproariously, he lurched into a semi-upright position and sent his pals off with shouted instructions.

"You better be back here to get me by ten!"

Loose-jointed and lanky with a long, lean face and smiling gray eyes, Kreger somehow looked less substantial than he was, both physically and mentally. Whirling around, he started for the building, only to halt when he clapped eyes on Chandler.

"My man!" he crowed, throwing wide his arms. "Get your dancing boots on, boy. We're celebrating!"

"No, thanks," Chandler said, turning away with the bags. Obviously, the celebration had already been going on for some time.

"You got to!" Pat insisted, stumbling forward to throw a chummy arm about Chandler's shoulder. His dark hair fell haphazardly across his forehead, and Chandler wondered where the man had left his hat this time. "You did it, old son," he slurred. "You won big, and so did I!"

"Funny," Chandler said, stepping away to escape the stench of alcohol, "I didn't realize you were even entered."

"Huh. There're other ways to make money on the rodeo," Kreger said, wagging a finger. "Bet on the big man, I told 'em. Not only has he got the goods, he's one of those blessed Chatams. And, brother, did you ever come through."

It made Chandler ill to think that his old partner had bet

on him. It seemed that Kreger was quickly spiraling downward. Chandler was surprised to feel some responsibility. Not only was he no longer around to pull his old partner out of trouble, but he also had obviously made no impression on Kreger with his Christian witness. He'd thought he was showing Kreger how to live by following him around and rescuing him from one mess or another. Now he knew that he'd only abetted Kreger's downfall. He suddenly wondered how many opportunities he had squandered. Why hadn't he just *told* his friend about Christ? Oh, he'd laid out his beliefs more than once, and Kreger had even paid lip service to the idea of Christianity, but that had been long ago. Chandler was ashamed now that he'd settled for that.

"Pat," he said kindly, "you need to sober up and think about what you're doing."

"Good old Chandler," Kreger drawled, "still trying to be my conscience. It's a wonder I never knocked your block off."

Bethany stepped around the end of the truck then, saying nervously, "Chandler?"

"It's okay. Nothing to worry about," he assured her calmly.

Beside him, Kreger's smoke-gray eyes were bugging out of his chiseled face. "Who's that with you? She's a looker even if she is knocked up."

Chandler dropped the bags and slammed Kreger against the truck before he realized what he was doing. He didn't know who was more surprised, him or Pat. Obviously, Chandler thought, he was having a little more trouble forgiving than he'd realized. Still, a point had to be made.

"That's my wife you're talking about," he said sharply, "so you watch your mouth."

Kreger's jaw dropped. "W-wife!"

"That's right. And don't you forget it."

Chandler stepped back, rolled his shoulders to ease the tension and picked up the bags again. Kreger was still plastered to the side of the truck when Chandler reached Bethany's side and glanced back.

She slid her arm through his, saying, "Let's go in. It's kind of chilly out here."

"Downright frosty," he agreed, though it was probably sixty degrees. The evening chill had less to do with the weather in the high desert than the company. He sent Kreger a hard look before picking up the bags and walking inside with Bethany, carrying their luggage and his regrets with him.

She wanted to talk about it as soon as they got into the room, but he didn't see what good that would do. Kreger was his past. She was his present. Matthew was his future. Besides, she was clearly exhausted, and they had to get up early in order to make it back to Buffalo Creek in time for Bethany's appointment with her obstetrician, which was scheduled for three o'clock in the afternoon.

"Let's just get some sleep," he told her.

Nodding, she went about her business in near silence and was out, so far as he could tell, almost as soon as her head hit the pillow. Chandler, however, spent a restless night, his delight at winning tempered by his run-in with Kreger.

He hated to see what his old friend had come to and hated the anger that still burned in his own heart, but change was a choice, one they each had to make for themselves. At least, Chandler thought, he had help. He had the awesome power and gentle—sometimes not-so-gentle—guidance of his Lord God.

Who, he wondered sadly, did Kreger have now?

Finally giving up the fight, Chandler rose before 5:00 a.m. and had them on the road within twenty minutes. Bethany, bless her, did her best not to hold up the process, but Chandler made sure to stop often. It was a near thing, though. They barely had time to drop off the horses at Dovey's before barreling across town to the doctor's office.

Chandler sat in the waiting room, one of only a pair of males in a building full of pregnant women, plugging numbers into his financial plan via his laptop. Seventeen thousand gave him a nice cushion, but it wouldn't pay for the upkeep of the horses, entry fees, even reduced, and travel expenses for very long, let alone rent and self-employment taxes. The cost of gasoline was eating him alive, what with his constant trips back and forth to Stephenville to practice with Drew. If he was careful, though, these winnings would see him through to the end of the year. If he was blessed with more winnings... That he could only leave in God's hands. At least he had a little breathing room now.

When Bethany came out after seeing the doctor, she seemed a bit subdued, and that immediately concerned Chandler. So, as he was walking her up into the truck, he asked if everything was okay.

"Oh, yes. It's just that I have to register at the hospital soon."

He knew what that meant, and he couldn't imagine why he hadn't thought of it before. So much for his financial plan. "In other words, you have to start paying on the hospital bill."

"I've saved for it," she told him, smiling. He wasn't fooled a bit. She'd been paying the doctor on her own. She couldn't possibly have the funds for the hospital bill.

Well, Lord, he thought, *I guess when You give me money that means You're preparing me for what's coming. So be it. We'll use Your plan.*

He drove her straight to the hospital, wrote a two-thousand-dollar check as a down payment and signed a paper agreeing to pay the same for a period of months to cover the estimated costs. Bethany cried about it on their walk across the parking lot.

"This is so unfair. I never meant for this to happen to you. Why didn't I realize this would happen to you?"

"Here now," he told her, reaching around her to open the passenger door of the truck. "No reason for tears. This is what a husband and daddy does."

She turned and threw her arms around his waist, laying her cheek in the hollow of his shoulder. "Oh, Chandler! You're so good to me. That's why I—"

His heart stopped. Everything in him hoped, believed, that she was about to declare her love. Hovering on the very verge of elation, he stood poised to exult. Suddenly he understood what really mattered. Losing the ranch and all that money, having to live with his elderly aunties, burning up the highway between Buffalo Creek and Stephenville, winning, what anyone else thought—none of that mattered. Getting himself right with God, *that* mattered. This woman in his arms, *she* mattered. His family, especially Bethany and Matthew, *they* mattered. Nothing else.

I finally understand, Lord, he thought, holding his breath, waiting for the words that would make his world come right at last.

"I—I'm so grateful," she finally whispered.

The disappointment was crushing. It felt as if a six-hundred-pound steer had rolled over him. And then kicked him in the head, for good measure.

After a moment, Chandler realized that he was patting her awkwardly. Clearing his throat, he croaked, "No need for that."

He dried her tears with the tail of his shirt before driving her home to Chatam House and the separate bedrooms that summed up their marriage—and his foolishness—very neatly.

* * *

"Don't mean to be a wet blanket," Chandler said to his aunts at the dinner table that night. "But it's been a really busy few days."

Magnolia traded glances with her sisters before putting on a smile for their nephew. "Of course, dear."

"Congratulations, again, and sleep well," Hypatia said from her chair at the head of the dark, ornately carved dining table.

"Good night!" Odelia called gaily as Chandler disappeared into the hallway. Bethany had gone up perhaps half an hour earlier. She hadn't even waited for dessert to be served, though Hilda had baked her favorite butterscotch-glazed chocolate cake that day.

"The weekend seems to have taken a toll on our newly-weds," Hypatia murmured after a moment.

"Bethany did look a bit peaked," Odelia worried aloud. She seemed uncharacteristically subdued herself today, dressed in filmy pale gray with black bows, about a dozen of them, from the enormous one atop her head to those that dangled from her earlobes and ran down the front of her dress.

"Chandler will see to Bethany," Magnolia stated with absolute certainty. She did not doubt that her nephew and his wife cared for each other. Unfortunately, she wasn't sure that they realized that fact themselves.

"Humph." Garrett pushed back his chair just to the left of Magnolia and got to his feet, tossing his napkin down beside his plate. While Bethany and Chandler had been away, he'd taken his meals with the rest of the staff, but tonight his sister had wanted him at the table in the formal dining room when she'd announced Chandler's big win. Garrett had been as congratulatory as everyone else, but he obviously had an issue. "Ask me, she shouldn't have been dragged off to that rodeo."

"But she wanted to go, dear," Magnolia pointed out.

"No doubt she did," Garrett conceded. "That doesn't mean she should have."

Magnolia disagreed, but she didn't argue the point. Garrett's brotherly concern was entirely reasonable, if a bit short-sighted. He seemed to think that the marriage was set in stone. The sisters were not so sure.

Garrett left the room. The sisters sat in their places, calmly eating last bites and drinking last sips while his footsteps faded down the hallway. Finished with her meal, Hypatia placed her heavy cutlery just so atop her dessert plate, while Odelia fussily folded her napkin. Magnolia simply waited until she couldn't wait anymore.

"So, what do you think?"

Odelia looked up, shaking her head mournfully. The black bows swung from her earlobes like clock pendulums.

"Patience," Hypatia counseled. "They are acting more and more like a committed couple."

"They have been spending a good deal of time together," Odelia noted hopefully.

"And Chandler did say that he wants Bethany to give up her job now," Hypatia noted.

"Something she obviously has no intention of doing," Magnolia pointed out.

She suspected that they had not been told everything that had taken place that weekend, which was as it should be. Much of marriage was private, after all. More worrisome than that was the problem of Garrett and what he might feel compelled to do if this marriage did not "take." Oh, she didn't expect violence, per se, but Garrett's record implied that it wouldn't be pretty if Chandler and Bethany split and Bethany was less than happy about it.

Sighing, Hypatia said, "I just wish Chandler didn't have so much on his plate."

"Poor thing," Odelia opined. "His best friend cheats him, so he loses his home, his father thinks he got Bethany in a family way before he married her, and the marriage isn't even really a marriage."

"Yet," Magnolia put in. She had determined to remain doggedly optimistic on the subject. "It may not be a real marriage *yet*."

"But at least he won!" Odelia finished happily.

"Obviously," Hypatia said, with a decisive nod, "God is at work."

"We can only wait," Magnolia counseled, "to see what He will do." Meanwhile, she would continue to pray. Ah, well, prayer was always a good thing.

One step forward, two steps back, Bethany thought, sighing as she neatened the papers on her desk. It had been a busy day. Tuesdays always were, but that didn't keep her from dwelling on the lamentable state of her marriage.

Last week had been wonderful. Chandler had seemed relaxed, attentive, smiling, and he'd won! She was so happy for him and so proud to be his wife. The hospital bill still mortified her, but he had been so generous and good about it.

"That is what a husband and daddy does."

She closed her eyes, remembering the thrill of delight that had swept through her at those words. And then she'd gone and ruined it all by almost blurting that she loved him.

He had to have known. Why else would he have pulled back like this? She'd felt it at once, and though she'd tried to recover by saying that she was grateful instead, he had instantly put emotional distance between them. Oh, he'd been polite, solicitous, even, but it was as if they lived on opposite sides of a wall now. She'd tried to breach the barrier by bragging on him at dinner that night, but he had seemed uncomfortable with the praise.

Disheartened and exhausted, she'd excused herself early and gone up to their suite. He had come up a little later and gone straight to his room with only the barest, "Good night," and he'd hardly spoken a word to her since.

What could she conclude except that he didn't reciprocate her feelings?

A cramp suddenly tightened Bethany's abdominal muscles, making her gasp. Hub crossed the foyer, pointing a young mother with a toddler on her hip toward the provision room, where she would be allowed to pick up disposable diapers and clothing for the child, having finished her parenting class. As soon as the girl, for she couldn't have been more than seventeen, had passed out of earshot, he turned back to Bethany's desk.

"What's wrong?"

She shook her head, but the cramp was taking its time. She gripped the edge of her desk with both hands and tried to breathe until her abdominal muscles finally relaxed. "I-It's nothing."

Hub frowned. "It doesn't look like nothing."

"It's just the Braxton-Hicks," she assured him, taking a clean breath and offering him a wobbly smile.

Clearly not convinced, he asked, "Should I call someone? Your doctor? Your brother? Chandler?"

"I'm fine," she told him. "And Chandler's in Stephenville today."

Hub made a face. "A married man has no business being on the road like this all the time. Who is this Drew Shaw that he keeps running off to see, anyway? Another Pat Kreger, probably."

Bethany snorted at that. "Hardly. Drew and Cindy Shaw are sweet, Christian people. The four of us prayed together before every go-round last weekend. And Cindy's expecting a baby in early November, so we have a lot in common. I think they're wonderful."

Hub's expression had gradually eased as she'd spoken, but all he said was, "Hmm." Then, "What's a go-round?"

Smiling inwardly, Bethany told him. She told him a lot more after that, including details of the Cowboy Church service and how magnificently Chandler had performed that weekend. Hub tried to appear only mildly interested, but he didn't fool her. He was soaking it all up like a sponge. Amazed that father and son had never sat down together and discussed these things, she prayed that before this marriage ended, she would see them do it. That, at least, would be something good that Chandler could take from their time together as husband and wife.

Sitting on the tailgate of the truck on Thursday evening, Chandler watched the sun sink slowly in the west, painting the dusky-blue sky in shades of yellow-gold, orange and red. He was tired to the bone, worn to an absolute nub, and he had a rodeo to get to.

He didn't want to go. For the first time in memory, he just did not want to think about getting on the road. Yet, he couldn't stay. If he didn't get away from the very woman who drew him like a lodestone, he was going to shatter into tiny pieces. It hurt to be in a room with her, to breathe the same air that she breathed, and no matter how much he prayed, it didn't change.

The whole thing had him confused. It was as if God had made her just for him. What woman could be better suited to or more understanding of his lifestyle? Who else would be so sweet and patient with all his traveling? He supposed it was too much to ask that she love him, too, especially after all she'd been through, but that didn't keep it from hurting.

The door opened and closed behind him. Bethany came out onto the stoop beneath the porte cochere, her arms folded as if against a chill.

"Dinner in half an hour," she said hesitantly. "Stuffed pork chops."

Chandler slid off the tailgate and shoved it closed. "Sounds good, but I'll have to pass. Tell the aunties and Hilda that I said thanks and that I apologize for not staying."

"Can't you eat first?"

"I need to get on my way."

"You need dinner, too."

"I'll grab something later."

"And eat behind the wheel while driving," she said, frowning with disapproval.

"Nothing I haven't done many a time," he replied, checking again to make sure that everything in the bed was lashed down.

"But why do it when you don't have to?" she pressed.

He heard himself snap, "Stop nagging me, Bethany!" Instantly contrite, he squeezed his eyes shut.

"I just want you to be safe," she said in a small voice.

Knowing that he'd been unfair, he tried to make amends. "I'm sorry. I didn't mean that. You never nag."

"I would if I thought it would do any good," she admitted, shocking a bark of laughter out of him.

"I'll be fine," he assured her. "I've been doing this on my own for a long time."

"You're not on your own anymore, though, Chandler," she pointed out softly.

"Aren't I?" he asked, suddenly angry again. "Barely married. That's what we are, Bethany." He held up his thumb and forefinger, squinting through the tiny space between them. "Just barely married. We didn't even speak our vows in church because we knew we didn't mean them. How's that not on my own anymore?"

She shifted uncertainly, looking so sadly adorable in that same blue-and-white-flowered sundress in which he'd first seen her that he could have cried.

"What are you saying, Chandler?"

What was he saying? Nothing that he wanted to say. Nothing that he should say. He shook his head. "I'm not saying anything, Bethany. I'm just in a foul mood today, that's all."

"Because of the money," she said morosely.

"Money?"

"For the hospital."

He hadn't thought of that at all. In fact, he hadn't been able to think of much of anything lately except her.

"No," he said, "it's not the money. Well, it is. I mean, I have to make a living, but the hospital bill's just part of that."

"A big part," she said, twisting her hands together. "I'm so sorry. After the baby comes, I'll find a full-time job and pay it back to you, I promise."

"Pay it back!" he erupted, all but shouting at her. "You're going to pay me back for providing for my own son? He is my son, isn't he, Bethany? That's what we agreed."

She stood there staring at him with those big blue eyes without saying a word, and he felt like the biggest heel on earth. He had to get out of there before he did something even worse, like spill his guts and lay his heart at her feet.

"I'm sorry," he said, starting around the truck. "I can't talk to you about this now. I have to go."

She ran to meet him, skirting around the front end of the truck. "Chandler!"

He got the door open before she reached him, and they drew up with that hunk of metal and glass between them, that and so much more. It wasn't enough. He didn't think anything could be. There could be light-years and aeons between them, and he'd still want her.

"I'll pray for you," she promised breathlessly. "Please be safe, and come home soon."

He reached for her before he could stop himself, his hands cupping her head through the dark silk of her hair and pulling her toward him. She bumped up against the door, belly first, her blue, blue eyes plumbing his. If only he knew what those eyes were telling to him.

It took every ounce of willpower he possessed not to bend his head and kiss her until the rest of the world just disappeared. Somehow, he managed to let go. Ducking into the truck cab, he slammed the door shut and reached for the keys.

She stood with her hands fisted beneath her chin as he backed the truck out from beneath the porte cochere and around the corner of the house, and she was the last thing that he saw in his rearview mirror before he turned the truck toward Dovey's and the longest, loneliest, saddest drive of his life.

Chapter Thirteen

Tears and prayer occupied Bethany's entire weekend. Even learning of Jay's lies had not frightened her like this. She'd been angry, yes, and hurt, but not afraid, not until he'd threatened to file for custody of the baby if she revealed his duplicity. She couldn't believe it had taken her so long to figure out his game.

Ironically, like Chandler, Jay had traveled for a living, supposedly as a paper goods salesman. She'd never known that, as Jason Widener, he possessed a controlling interest in the Houston paper goods distributor for which he supposedly worked. That was where he'd gotten the idea for his second persona, Jay Carter. Likewise, she was unaware that he owned a thriving real estate development business in Tulsa and had a second—or rather, a first—wife and family there.

The scam had been so simple, really. He carried two cell phones. One was supposedly for business use, the other for personal. She had called, used and answered the personal one many times over the years. She had never touched the other the phone, which he had kept on his person at all times, even carrying it into the bathroom with him when he showered.

Then she'd discovered that she was pregnant. He'd dragged his feet about having children, and she hadn't planned it, expecting that eventually his feelings would change, but suddenly they were going to have a baby. She was shocked by his anger. They argued about it incessantly every moment that he was there, which was less and less often. One morning he'd slammed out of the house in a rage over her determination to go through with the pregnancy, leaving his business phone behind. Almost at once, the thing had begun ringing insistently. Finally, concerned that it might be important or that it was him calling, Bethany had answered.

A woman on the other end of the line went berserk. Every word was permanently implanted in Bethany's brain.

"Who are you? Where's my husband? I knew he was having an affair! I knew it! He's a married man, you hussy! Have you no shame? Do you even think about our children?"

Stunned, she'd hung up without a word. She was throwing up when Jay returned, shocked into physical illness. It had taken her almost twenty-four hours to digest the full reality of her situation—and ten minutes to leave. Jay had first tried to convince her to "let things be," but as she'd packed her bags, he'd snarled that he would not let her ruin him and warned that no man would ever want her now.

"If you just hadn't insisted on having that kid!" he'd shouted.

Hours later she'd stumbled into Chandler's path. He had seemed God-given. She still believed it. He was the best thing that had ever happened to her, the best thing that could have happened for her son. And she was losing him. How could that be?

With that on her mind, when the phone rang in the suite late Sunday evening, Bethany literally recoiled. She never answered the phone at Chatam House, leaving that to the staff and the aunties. Besides, she'd never received a phone call there and didn't expect to, so she was surprised when

Magnolia tapped on her door a few minutes later to ask her to pick up.

Hurrying to the desk, she reached for the wireless receiver, then paused in concern before carrying it to the sofa. An unexpected phone call had destroyed her world once before. Was history about to repeat itself?

Warily, she pushed the green button and held the receiver to her head. "Hello?"

A gusty sigh greeted her. "Sorry if I got you out of bed."

It was Chandler, and the sound of his voice both warmed and chilled her.

"No, no. I—I haven't gotten there yet."

"That's good," he said. Then, "No, actually, that's bad. You need your sleep."

"I'll sleep when you're home again," she said thoughtlessly.

A long silence followed, then softly Chandler said, "Honey, that's why I'm calling. I won't be in tonight. I broke an axle on the trailer, and it'll be tomorrow before I can find someone to repair it."

"Are you all right?" she asked shakily.

"I'm fine," he insisted. "Horses, too. But we aren't going anywhere until I get these wheels turning, and this is the back of beyond up here in Colorado. Drew's with me, though. Cindy didn't come this trip, either."

"Is there anything I can do?"

"Just keep praying. You must have some pull, girl. We did fine up here. Purse is not as large as last time, but what there was, we two walked away with. One of the fellas joked that we were in an all-fired hurry this weekend, and Drew said it was 'cause we couldn't wait to get home to our women." He laughed lightly, while Bethany's heart clutched. "He's right about that. Fact is, I miss you." Belatedly he added, "I-It's not half so fun without you and Cindy."

"Oh, Chandler, I miss you, too," she managed, her throat suddenly clogged.

"Bethany, I'm sorry about the way I left," he said, his entire tone changing. "I've got a bit of a temper, as you know. You've seen me and my dad go at it a couple times now. I didn't mean to take my frustration out on you. You've done nothing wrong, and you're more dear to me than you probably realize. It's just this lousy temper of mine."

She laughed as tears rolled down her cheeks. "If you call that a lousy temper, Chandler Chatam, then you know nothing of real anger. Now, my stepfather had a bad temper. A little moodiness now and again is a birthday party compared to that. Besides, you have a right to your frustration. I've complicated your life terribly."

"It's gotten real interesting, I admit," he told her, but there was a smile in his voice. "I was doing a good job of complicating things on my own before you came along, though. And I like your complications a whole lot better than mine."

She laughed again, then bit her lip as a painful cramp hit her. They'd been coming every few hours, each seemingly more vicious than the last, and her back ached constantly these days. The former was no doubt a measure of her emotional stress, the latter a result of the extra weight she was carrying. She promised herself that she was going to stop worrying now and trust God to take care of things. That would surely take care of the cramps if not the backache.

"I'll call you tomorrow when I know what's what," Chandler promised. "You get some sleep now."

"I will," she said, trying not to let on as the cramp rolled through her. "C-congratulations on your wins. Wish I could have been there."

"Me, too," he whispered. "Night."

"Good night."

Breaking the connection, she laid her head back. As her

muscles gradually relaxed, she dried her eyes and smiled. She had feared the unexpected call for no reason.

The most important bits played through her mind.

You're more dear to me than you probably realize. I miss you.

It was a start, she told herself. Good things could come at the end of a telephone line, too. Even with a broken axle to be mended and the necessary delay in his return, Chandler's call had given her more peace and hope than any other ever had.

"Keep praying," he'd said, and that was just what she was going to do. She'd pray her husband safely home and her way straight into his heart.

Chandler backed the trailer into the barn and killed the engine of the truck. Behind him, the horses bumped against the metal walls, eager to get out and chow down. He didn't blame them. What a rough few days it had been! He'd slept in his truck two nights in a row to safeguard his horses, sending Drew off home as soon as he'd found someone to replace the axle. That had taken an entire day, though, so here he was on a Tuesday afternoon just now getting back to Buffalo Creek.

Thankfully, he had won a good bit, enough so that the four hundred bucks he'd spent getting back on the road hadn't troubled him. In fact, he'd promised God and himself that he wasn't going to worry about the money anymore. They'd make do with whatever God provided.

He wasn't even going to worry anymore about moving out of Chatam House. When the timing was right, it would happen. Meanwhile, he could hardly complain about the accommodations. It was mostly a matter of pride with him, anyway. He was learning to swallow that when he had to.

He'd swallowed a bit of it when he'd called Bethany, and he was glad he had.

As soon as he could work his courage up to it, he was going to tell her how he really felt and hope that it wasn't just her sweetness and misplaced guilt that had made her act as she had. He'd been thinking about the way she'd said that she missed him and other things—incessantly. It could be wishful thinking on his part, but it seemed to him that there was at least hope that her feelings had changed. And even if they had not, they still could. Maybe just letting her know that he wanted her to love him, that he wanted this marriage to work, would be enough to start the ball rolling. Whatever the outcome, though, he had to try.

The worst that could happen, after all, was what he already had, a temporary marriage in name only. If that was what God willed, Chandler decided, then God would undoubtedly make a way for him to survive it.

He off-loaded the horses, walked them into their stalls and began hauling out the feed. He didn't bother with the wheelbarrow as the truck was in the way. His phone rang as he carried the heavy bag toward the stalls, balancing it on one shoulder. He fished the phone out of his shirt pocket with one hand and glanced at the caller ID. Frowning, he tried to remember the last time his father had called him. That had surely been the day Kaylie and Stephen had gotten engaged, though Hub's intent at the time had been to derail such a possibility by convincing her brothers to oppose the romance. Curious, Chandler answered the call.

"What's up, Dad?"

"Are you in town?"

"I'm just dropping off the horses."

"Thank God!"

Chandler's heart stopped. "Why? What's wrong?"

"Best come to the hospital, son. Bethany's in labor."

Chandler didn't wait to hear more. He dropped the bag of feed and sprinted for the rig, one hand clamped to the crown of his hat. He was in the cab before he remembered that he hadn't put up the ramp and locked down the trailer door. Barking questions at his dad, he hurriedly went about securing the trailer and jumped back into the truck.

According to Hub, Bethany had complained of cramps and nausea earlier in the day. He'd tried to convince her to go home, but she'd insisted on lying down on the sofa in the counseling room. When Hub had checked on her some time later, he'd found her holding her belly and moaning. He'd gotten her up and walked her to his car, intending to drive her to her doctor's office. She'd argued that she was merely suffering from Braxton-Hicks contractions—right up to the moment that she'd doubled over and screamed. Hub had rushed her to the emergency room. He had no idea what was happening with her now, as they wouldn't let him stay with her.

Lights flashing, Chandler raced through town, trailer and all, laying on his horn at intersections and praying fervently aloud.

"Oh, Lord, let it be another false alarm. It's too early, and she's all alone in there. Please just take care of them. Protect them both. Please don't let me lose either of them!"

He left the rig at the curb in a no-parking zone. Let them ticket him. Let them tow the whole kit and kaboodle! He didn't care. If his wife and son were not well, then nothing else mattered. Dashing inside to the elevators, he caught a car just as the door was closing on an elderly fellow carrying a pot plant. The old gentleman nodded, but Chandler was too overwrought to return the greeting. He poked the elevator button repeatedly, in the faint hope that it would somehow speed up the seemingly interminable ride.

At last, the elevator came to a halt and the door slid open.

Chandler bolted for the nurses' station. A heavyset, fortyish woman with a long, thin brown ponytail looked up and smiled at him.

"Where's my wife?" Chandler demanded.

The woman had obviously seen too many distraught husbands to pay much attention to them. "Name?"

"Bethany Chatam."

The nurse didn't even check her records before glancing up and saying, "They're on their way down with her now."

"Down?"

"Delivery is on the next floor."

"She's had the baby, then?"

"She has."

Stunned, Chandler babbled, "I-Is the baby okay?"

To his dismay, the nurse looked away, saying, "The doctor's with him now."

Chandler gulped and swept off his hat, remembering only then that it was still on his head. "I have to see Bethany."

The nurse gave him the room number and told him that he could wait there. He went straight to the room. The space contained a sitting area complete with sofa and recliner, as well as a private bath and flat-screen TV. It had everything except a bed. Tossing his hat onto the sofa, he paced the floor for several seconds before the door opened and his father walked in.

"Dad! Where is she?"

"She'll be along any minute."

"How is she?"

Hub hitched his pants up around his paunch, his frame otherwise so thin that he often joked that he looked like an olive on a toothpick. His expression lacked any hint of amusement, however. "Physically, she's fine. Doctor said she had a quick, easy time of it, though she's probably been in what he called slow labor for a couple days. It was obvious this morning that she didn't feel good. Still, she seemed to think it would pass until almost the very end."

"You said she's okay *physically*."

"Yes. Emotionally…" Hub shook his head.

"It's the baby, isn't it? What are they saying about him?"

Hub sighed. "I gather there are some problems. The doctor said something about babies losing weight during protracted labors like this and stress delaying development."

Feeling as if his legs might buckle, Chandler stumbled backward. "I—I don't know what I'll do if anything happens to either of them."

Hub reached out and clapped a supporting hand on Chandler's shoulder, saying, "Put your faith in God, son. He'll see you through."

Chandler nodded. "I know. I know. It's just…I should've been here! I've mucked up everything."

Placing both hands on Chandler's shoulders, Hub captured his gaze and held it for a long moment before softly saying, "No. No, you haven't. In fact, I'd say you've done very well. The fact is, I'm proud of you, Chandler."

Chandler shook his head. He'd waited a long time to hear that, but now that it had been said, it hurt more than it helped, for he knew the truth. "No, no. I—I've been holding out on God, Dad. It's not just that I refused to see what Kreger was doing. I enabled him. And I've been so angry, blaming him for everything, when the truth is that I'm as responsible for how it all turned out as he was. I didn't take care of my business, and I wasn't the man, the Christian, I should have been. You were right about that, too." He looked his father in the eye then, confessing all, "And the very worst part is that I never found a way to bring Pat around. I didn't even *try*. I never once told him, point-blank, what Christ did for him, for me."

Hub gulped, his chin trembling. "I may have been right

about Patrick Kreger," he said, "but I was wrong about you, and neither case pleases me." Hub clamped his hands down hard on Chandler's shoulders, saying, "You're a better man than I realized. Bethany told me, you see. She didn't mean to. She was frightened and in pain, and she cried out that she wished you really were her baby's father."

"But I am!" Chandler insisted, alarmed. She wouldn't go back on that now, would she? He thought wildly that there had to be some way to keep that from happening.

"Of course you're his father," Hub agreed, nodding. "By choice. She told me everything. When the whole town, me included, I'm ashamed to say, just assumed you were the father, you could have denied it, but that would have exposed her to criticism, so you kept quiet. You could have walked away at any time and been fully justified in doing so, but you *chose* to give Bethany and Matthew your name and protection."

But he hadn't chosen to give them his heart. That had just happened.

The door swung open again, and Garrett rushed in.

"How is she?"

"I called him after I called you," Hub explained. "Bethany asked me to, in case you were still on the road."

Chandler told him what little he knew. Garrett made a fist and smacked it into his other palm. "If I could get my hands on that Jay Carter…"

"You know?" Chandler said, surprised.

Garrett sent him a sideways look. "I figured it out. What I'm not sure about is why you stepped into his shoes."

"I'll explain it for you, then," Chandler replied smartly, "right after I explain it to your sister."

The door opened once more. Chandler pushed past his father and brother-in-law as the head of a hospital bed appeared, only to step back again as the bed rolled into the room and a man in green scrubs maneuvered it into position. Bethany lay there, shivering and silently weeping.

The first words out of her mouth were, "I didn't get to see him! They wouldn't even let me see Matthew before they took him!"

"It'll be all right, sis," Garrett offered, but she ignored him, her gaze fixed on Chandler.

"I'm so glad you're here. I'm so frightened!"

Fear unlike anything Chandler had ever felt before swamped him, but he went to the bed smiling as brightly as he could manage and bent to smooth back her damp hair and kiss her clammy forehead. "Garrett's right, sweetheart. Everything's going to be okay."

"If I could just see him."

"We'll see our little Matthew soon, I promise."

Two nurses, the heavyset one and another who was quite young, swept into the room. Chandler took Bethany's hand, his thumb smoothing over the cool surface of her wedding band. He stayed at her side while the nurses did their thing, then before they left he asked, "Can you tell us about our son? When can we see him?"

"The doctor will be in," the heavyset one said tersely.

Bethany immediately began to sob.

Chandler looked at her crumpled face and made an instant decision. "Forget that." Bending, he scooped her up, bedcovers and all, and started for the door. "Where is he? We want to see our son right now."

The nurses went into a tizzy of scolding and urging, but he couldn't even hear them. "Right now," he repeated.

Garrett pulled open the door. Hub pointed the direction. With Bethany clinging to his neck, Chandler carried her out into the wide, gleaming hall, both nurses hot on his heels. The older one turned toward the nurses' desk. The other ran past them toward a solid metal door.

Behind him, Chandler heard his father whisper, "Gracious Lord God, please, I beg You…"

Chandler joined his prayers to his father's as he strode after the nurse. He couldn't bear the thought of losing little Matthew now, and neither could he bear the pain and fear of this woman who held his heart.

Chapter Fourteen

The nurse turned to face them as if she would physically block their path. Chandler prepared to bully his way past her, if necessary, but then her brow beetled, and she swiped the ID card hanging about her neck through a card reader on the wall.

"Thank You," he whispered, knowing Who had surely changed her mind.

The wide door swung open, the edge coming to rest next to a sign that detailed the nursery visiting hours. Chandler didn't even bother reading it. Instead, he strode through that door and followed the nurse, Bethany cradled against his chest.

The frantic nurse hurried past a pair of large windows with blinds drawn and went through a smaller door marked, "Medical Personnel Only." Chandler went after her, catching the heavy door before it swung closed.

Another woman in scrubs and a puffy cap rushed toward him. "Sir! Sir! You cannot come in here!"

"I can if my son's in here. Where is he?"

Chandler looked around, turning in a wide circle in what

was essentially a glass-walled hallway. The clear plastic cribs in the viewing room were all empty, though several showed signs of recent habitation. Those infants were probably with their mothers at that moment. In fact, so far as Chandler could see, there were only two infants currently in residence. One, a squalling girl, if the pink wristband was any indication, was being weighed. The other was ominously silent, a pale, tiny body in a closed, brightly lit incubator in a separate room. A young man with a dark complexion and a long lab coat came to the door and nodded them over. He introduced himself as the pediatrician and led them to the incubator.

Pulling a hard plastic chair forward, the doctor informed them, "He's small and jaundiced and his lungs are not fully developed."

Chandler stood for a moment with Bethany in his arms, staring at the tiny, wrinkled body covered with tubes and tape and a tiny diaper that seemed much too large. Chandler bit his lips, but still the tears trickled down his cheeks. Swallowing, he managed to say to Bethany, "He has your dark hair."

Bethany reached out a hand, touching the incubator. "Why are his eyes covered?"

"To protect them against the light." The doctor explained that phototherapy was used to help the bilirubin in the blood break down so the body could eliminate it. The feeding and hydration tubes would increase eliminations, as well as help the baby gain weight. At four pounds, he could use the help! A third tube was used to inject medication to help with the development of the lungs.

"Is he going to make it?" Bethany asked in a quivering voice.

"He'll make it," Chandler said, clutching her tighter.

"We'll know within twenty-four to forty-eight hours," the doctor answered honestly. "If he loses ground, we'll transfer him to an NICU in a larger hospital."

"He'll make it," Chandler decreed flatly.

"I've seen smaller, sicker babies pull through," the doctor went on, "but it depends on his organ development." Indicating the chair, he added, "If you'll wait thirty or forty minutes, you can hold him."

Chandler sat down in the chair with Bethany in his lap. She laid her head on his shoulder, and he kissed her temple. She closed her eyes, but Chandler knew that she wasn't resting; she was praying. He pressed his cheek to the crown of her head, closed his eyes and joined his heart to hers, as together they silently begged for the life and well-being of their son.

An hour later, Chandler followed as a floor nurse wheeled Bethany back to her room. He hadn't wanted to let her go, but the nurse had quietly insisted. Bethany had eased off Chandler's lap and into the wheelchair without a word, her gaze following little Matthew as the neonatal technician returned him to the incubator, reconnected his tubes, covered his eyes. He seemed lethargic and weak to Chandler, and the fear that had lodged itself in his chest would not ease.

Once they reached the room, Chandler lifted Bethany from the chair and tucked her safely into bed. "I had to see him," she whispered, clasping Chandler's hand.

She, too, seemed alarmingly weak, completely exhausted. "Of course. Rest now. Everything's going to be okay."

Bethany closed her eyes, and Chandler moved toward his father and Garrett, who sat side by side on the sofa. The nurse came in then, the young one who had opened the security door for them. Chandler caught her by the sleeve.

"Thank you," he said simply.

Nodding, she moved toward the bed and made Bethany swallow pills. Hub rose then. Garrett followed suit an instant later.

"We'll go so she can rest."

"Will you tell the aunties and everyone for us?"

"Spoke to them a while ago," Garrett said. "Everyone sends their love."

"Thanks."

"I'll be praying for you all, son."

"Never doubted it for a minute. Counting on it, in fact."

Hub patted Chandler's arm, then went to the bed and bent to kiss Bethany's brow. "Don't you worry now."

"I'll try not to," she murmured wearily.

Garrett took his turn, hugging her and kissing her cheek. "I'll check on you later. Call if you need anything."

Bethany nodded and closed her eyes.

"I'll take care of her," Chandler said.

Garrett smiled wanly. "I know you will." He shifted his weight and admitted, "I had my doubts, but not anymore." With that, he moved toward the door.

Hub followed, but then he paused and turned back. "I wasn't right about Kreger," he said. "To have been right, I'd have had to do everything in my power to win that boy to the Lord, but I was too busy blaming him for pulling you away from me."

"And I was too busy defending and using him," Chandler admitted. "This is a failure we share."

"Then it's one we'll have to rectify together," Hub said. "We'll pray, and when the time is right, we'll go together to speak to Kreger. He needs to know that God loves him."

Chandler nodded, his eyes swimming. "I'd like that."

Hub smiled and left them.

Chandler pulled the recliner around, took Bethany's limp hand in his and sat down at her side, where he wanted always to be.

Watching the nurse return Matthew to the incubator, Bethany wearily sat back in the chair. Most babies stayed in their mothers' rooms, but all through the night, she and Chandler had made the journey down the hallway to the nearly empty nursery to hold and talk to Matthew. They'd tried to doze between visits, but neither of them had gotten any real sleep, and it showed.

Chandler pushed away from the wall and reached for her hand, pulling her up to her feet. He looked like she felt, much the worse for wear. His hair was mussed and falling over his forehead, and he needed a shave, his beard glinting dark gold in the light. His clothing, a faded green, long-sleeved, button-down shirt and jeans, was rumpled and creased. She thought him the most handsome man she'd ever seen.

Sliding his arm about her shoulders, he urged her toward the door. Her head felt so heavy that she wouldn't have been surprised if it fell off and rolled across the floor, so she laid it on Chandler's shoulder, wrapping an arm around his waist. They walked out of the nursery and down the hall to her room, where someone named Kelli had signed her name with a smiley face in the place of the dot over the *i* on the whiteboard mounted on the wall. Apparently, the nursing shift had changed.

Bethany's breakfast tray sat upon the rolling bed table; the congealing food looked anything but appealing. Chandler announced that he would go down to the cafeteria for something more tasty. He took the tray with him.

Bethany made herself go into the bathroom to clean up. She brushed her teeth, then swiftly washed her hair by bending over the tub and using the handheld showerhead. Feeling better, she dressed in the frilly pink nightgown and flowered robe that Garrett had brought her the previous evening and sat on the edge of the bed to comb out her hair. She had just put away the comb and climbed into the bed when the mysterious Kelli came in with a laptop computer and a printer on a small rolling stand.

As she plugged in her equipment, the young nurse explained that, though the state required birth certificates be filed within five days, hospital policy dictated that the paperwork be done within twenty-four hours. She had already input the data required of the hospital. Once she got Bethany's information, she would print the form and witness Bethany's signature. After the doctor signed, the hospital would file with the state.

Bethany settled back and answered several questions, her own name, age, place of birth and address. Chandler returned then with hot coffee, cold milk, fresh fruit and quiche.

"Can't get that served on the floor," Kelli noted with a wry smile before turning back to her business. "Father's full name?"

Bethany opened her mouth, but the words did not come out. All she could think was that the moment of no return had arrived. If Chandler's name went on that birth record, he would forever be committed to Matthew. It just didn't seem fair and at the very same time wasn't nearly enough to keep from breaking her heart. Helplessly, she looked to him, and found that he had frozen in the act of arranging their food on the bed table, an expression of wary disbelief on his face.

"Bethany," he urged softly.

The nurse spoke up. "I should have said, 'husband's full name.'"

"Hubner Chandler Chatam the third," Chandler said loudly.

"You'll have to spell that."

"H-u-b-n-e-r C-h-a-n-d-l-e-r C—"

"That's okay, I've got the Chatam part." She winked at Bethany, adding, "Everyone in Buffalo Creek can spell Chatam."

Gulping, Bethany asked, "What if the husband is n-not the f-father?"

"Bethany!" Chandler hissed.

She looked up, tears in her eyes. "It's just not fair for you to take on all this responsibility!"

"Honey, don't do this," Chandler urged softly. Glancing at the nurse, he reminded her, "HIPAA laws prevent you from revealing anything about your patients, right?"

"Absolutely." She cleared her throat and briskly informed them, "In Texas, the husband's name always goes on the birth certificate. If the mother is unmarried, she alone names the father. Anyone who disagrees has to file a paternity suit."

Bethany closed her eyes. So, it was already too late. She had unknowingly locked Chandler into fatherhood that day in the office of the Justice of the Peace in Oklahoma.

"What have I done?" she whispered. It would be different if he loved her, if the marriage was real, instead of the kind act of a truly caring and generous man.

"You've given me a son," Chandler answered softly.

"And me a grandson," said another familiar voice. Bethany opened her eyes to find a whole host of people filing into the room, Hub in the lead. He had his Bible in hand and a smile on his face.

"And us another nephew," Magnolia stated firmly, coming to stand between her sisters at the foot of the bed. She carried a vase full of flowers, naturally. Hypatia held a small, sturdy basket by the handle. Its contents, covered by a white cloth, gave off a mouthwatering aroma. Odelia, Bethany couldn't help noticing, was dressed in baby blue with little stick people dangling from her earlobes and a baby rattler corsage pinned to her chest. She held a blue-and-yellow gift bag, as if they hadn't already given her and Matthew enough! Kaylie carried another.

"Uh, I believe that's grandnephew," pointed out a dignified-looking man with twinkling eyes. Handsome and urbane, with streaks of gray at his temples, he had the Chatam chin, as did the older, rotund fellow in expensive pinstripes next to him.

"My brothers Morgan and Bayard," Chandler said, waving a hand between them. Bayard, a banker who lived in Dallas, had to be the heavy, older one. Morgan, as Chandler had told her, was a history professor at Buffalo Creek Bible College.

Morgan went on speaking to Magnolia, "Matthew Chandler would be your grand-nephew and *our* nephew."

A tall, grinning young man who was undoubtedly Kaylie's hockey-playing husband, Stephen, leaned forward and cheekily remarked, "I believe he's *my* nephew as well, if only by marriage."

"Well, *I'm* blood kin," Garrett said, pushing past him to the bedside.

"Good grief," Chandler said with obviously feigned disgust, "we've brought the whole family down on us."

"Hardly," Hypatia retorted with a chortle. "Just the immediate, as you well know."

The nurse wisely unplugged her equipment and beat a hasty retreat. Hub, too, slipped away, Bethany noticed.

"We apologize for interrupting your breakfast," Hypatia said.

"That's okay. We can eat later," Bethany told her.

"No, no." Morgan flipped back the cloth covering the contents of the basket in Hypatia's hands. "Go ahead and eat. We'll join you."

"Hilda's ginger muffins!" Stephen exclaimed, reaching over to snatch one.

Everyone began to help themselves. They all got comfortable, the aunties on the sofa, others leaning against the wall or sitting on the foot of the bed. Chandler sat down on the recliner next to the bed and wolfed down his own breakfast with his usual gusto, while Bethany worked on hers and listened to the chitchat. She recalled that Morgan and Bayard were the sons of Hub's first wife, who had been deceased many years now, whereas Kaylie and Chandler were the children of Hub's second wife, also deceased. That reminded Bethany that she'd seen Hub slip away.

Leaning toward Chandler, she asked, "Where's your father?"

He looked around. "Don't know."

Hypatia spoke up from the sofa. "I'm sure he'll return shortly."

Perhaps another quarter hour passed before Hub did so. He was not alone. A strange doctor followed carrying Matthew.

"Oh!" Bethany bolted straight up in the bed, holding out her arms. The doctor came over to place the baby in them.

"That's better," Hub said complacently, as everyone else "oohed" and "aahed" over Matthew.

Chandler shifted up to sit on the side of the bed next to Bethany, looking to the doctor. "I suppose you pulled rank on someone in order to manage this."

"Not at all. I just consulted with the neonatologist, at your father's request, and we made a decision based on the conditions and needs of both baby and mother."

"Thank you," Chandler said. He introduced the man to Bethany then, saying, "Honey, this is Brooks Leland, an old family friend."

"We spoke on the telephone," Bethany said, nodding to the newcomer.

Hub spoke up then. "All right, everyone, gather around. Gather around." The family all came to encircle the bed. "We're going to pray this new addition to our family home," Hub explained.

Holding her baby in her arms, Bethany looked around at them in amazement. These people weren't even really kin to her child, and she could see that they knew it, but here they all were on a Friday morning to pray over him just as if he truly did belong to them. Suddenly she knew that Matthew was exactly where he belonged. No matter who Matthew's biological father might be, His spiritual Father had brought them to his *true* father, to a true family. She would never question that again. Silently, she transferred Matthew into his father's arms.

Chandler jerked slightly in surprise, as he had not yet held his son. For a long moment, his gaze melded with hers. Then he tucked the tiny babe into the crook of one arm and looped his other about Bethany. Dressed in a tiny white gown, knit cap and blue blanket, Matthew stretched, mewled and turned his face into his father's chest. Beaming, Chandler glanced around the room.

Everyone shifted closer, laying hands on her or Chandler or little Matthew himself, and then they all bowed their heads as Hub began to pray aloud. He praised God for this new little family unit and thanked Him for the blessing of new beginnings. Finally, he beseeched God for Matthew's health, asking that the child thrive and grow and always be surrounded by the love of family and Christ Jesus. A chorus of Amens followed. Then Chandler dropped a delicate kiss on Matthew's cheek and smiled at Bethany.

"Well, that just leaves one other matter to attend," Hub announced, waving his Bible at Chandler and Bethany. "It's high time to bless this union properly. The legalities are one thing, but spiritualities are another." He lifted his sagging, cleft chin, adding, "And no child of mine is truly wed unless I officiate."

Bethany felt an instant of stomach-dropping panic, but Chandler's arm tightened about her shoulders, prompting her to look at him. She was stunned by the openness in his eyes, by the softness of his expression.

"I want this," he said quietly. "It won't be forever until he says the words. And that's what I want with you, forever. I know I don't have a lot to offer you right now, but I love you, Bethany, you and Matthew, and I believe with all my heart that the same God who brought you to me will provide all our needs." He looked down at her with such tenderness, their child cradled against him, that she lifted a hand to stifle an exclamation.

He was, essentially, asking her to marry him, to really marry him. For always. It was exactly what she wanted, but how could he possibly love her? Jay's insidious voice whispered that no man would want her, but when Chandler looked at her with those warm brown eyes of his, she knew that Jay lied. Again. She didn't know whether to laugh or to cry, so she did both.

Wrapping her arms about Chandler's neck, she twisted against him and whispered into his ear, "I love you so much. I love you so much!"

He buried his face in the bend of her neck, and she felt him sigh, the air leaving him in a long exhalation of relief. Lifting his head, he pressed a fervent kiss to her lips.

"It's always the cart before the horse with this one!" Hub joked good-naturedly.

Everyone laughed at that, including Bethany.

"Well, get it done, then," Chandler retorted smartly.

"Right now?" Hub asked. "You don't want to shave or at least comb your hair first?"

"I don't want to wait another minute," Chandler said. He abruptly turned back to Bethany then. "Oh, but maybe you would prefer a ceremony with all the trimmings this time?"

She looked down at herself. Here she sat in a hospital bed, her hair still damp from a cursory scrubbing, as exhausted as she'd ever been in her life. She must look a fright. Moreover, she'd been through two wedding ceremonies already, both elopements. With Jay Carter, the whole thing had been a farce. The second time had been legal, at least, but she had never dared to think that the marriage was true, never expected it to be more than a temporary favor done her by a good man who had rescued her out of nothing more than necessity and Christian sensibility. Now that darling man had declared his love and offered her a genuine marriage, a forever marriage, witnessed by those dearest to them. Trimmings were nothing compared to that.

"You've got to be kidding," she said, squeezing Chandler's hand.

He planted a kiss in the middle of her forehead. Then he dropped a frown on Matthew, one brow arching, and muttered, "Better make it quick. I think I have a diaper to change."

Everyone laughed at that. But no one laughed minutes later when Chandler and Bethany repeated their vows, there in the midst of their extended family, and received the blessing that joined their hearts forever as husband and wife.

It had been a strange and unexpected journey from that little diner beside the road to home and family and the fulfillment of all her dreams, but looking back on it now, Bethany knew that God had directed her path from the very moment that she had placed herself in His hands. She wished she had been wise enough to understand what He was doing, but she found it difficult to have regrets now, sitting there in the bosom of her expanded family with her loving husband and beautiful son beside her. In fact, she would do it all again just to arrive here at this wonderful place. And she could hardly wait to see where God would take them next.

Epilogue

Chandler crept into the bedroom, his boots in his hand. Bethany had left the light on in the bathroom and the door slightly ajar. He set the boots at the foot of the bed that had belonged to his grandparents and smiled down on his sleeping wife before tiptoeing to the cradle. Even after a month, Bethany preferred to keep Matthew close. Chandler preferred that, too. It had become more and more difficult to leave them both behind when he traveled to rodeos.

Drew felt the same way about Cindy, who was stuck at home awaiting the birth of their child, the slowpoke, as Chandler had taken to calling him, just to tease Drew, since Matt had made such an early entry. They were a pathetic pair, he and his partner, constantly thinking of those at home. Pathetic but successful, wildly so in the past few weeks, praise God!

No longer an infant scarecrow, Matthew had filled out well in the past few weeks. As Chandler stood there and marveled, Matt's plump little face scrunched up. His fists rose to bat about his head in the instant before he let out a full-throated wail. Chandler snatched him up, cradling him against his shoulder.

"Here, here," he whispered. "It's okay. Daddy's home."

Matthew crammed his fist into his mouth and continued to insist that he be fed. Chandler couldn't help chuckling. This was a boy in a hurry. Couldn't wait to be born, couldn't wait to get home from the hospital—a feat he'd managed only four days after Bethany—couldn't wait to grow, couldn't wait to eat, couldn't wait for clean britches. Just a sprinkle in his diaper was enough to set him off. Neither of his parents minded in the least.

Bethany groggily sat up and started to throw the covers off, but then she saw Chandler and smiled.

"Welcome home."

He bounced the fussing baby against his shoulder. "Glad to be here."

She held out her arms. "Let me have him before he wakes the whole household."

Chandler carried the little howler to the bed and watched in amazement as Bethany quieted him by holding him to her breast. She looked up, love shining in her bright blue eyes, and Chandler bent to kiss her, long and sweetly.

"I missed you, too," she said when he finally lifted his head. "How did it go?"

He fished a gold-plated buckle from his shirt pocket and tossed it on the bed, then pulled two more from his jeans and dropped those next to the first. Bethany gaped.

"Three?"

"Three events, three buckles," he said, grinning. "They'll fit better in a display case than three saddles."

She laughed and reached for his hand. "I'm so proud of you."

That meant more to him than anything else in the world. Chandler nudged her over with his hip and perched on the edge of the bed beside her.

"If we keep this up, Drew and I could make the national finals in December," he told her. "I might even qualify in steer wrestling. Tie-down's out of reach, though."

"This year," she said, and he smiled at her optimism. She glanced down at Matthew and commented, "We ought to be able to travel by December."

Chandler grinned. "Well, I'll see what I can do, then." They laughed together, then he sobered. "Speaking of December, I'd like us to be in our own place before the holidays."

She squeezed his hand. "Yes, I'd like that, too." It had been suggested that Chandler and Bethany move into Hub's house once he, Kaylie and Stephen moved out. "Your dad's house will be empty as soon as Kaylie finds something for them to lease." The house Kaylie was building with Stephen wouldn't be finished for at least another six months.

"I have another thought," Chandler said carefully. "What would you think about moving to Stephenville?"

Bethany lifted her eyebrows. "It would certainly make things a lot easier for you and Drew."

"We'd have more time to work, but more important I'd have more time to spend at home with you and Matthew," Chandler pointed out.

"A big plus."

He smiled, excitement welling up. "There's something else."

"Oh?"

"I had an offer on Ébano this weekend. Sixty-five thousand." She gasped. "I countered at eighty-five," he hurried on.

"And?"

"We split the difference at seventy-five thousand dollars."

"Chandler!"

"And I'm to train two other horses for the same fellow. If that works out, we might go into a partnership on the other end of things, so to speak. Then I'd be working with the horses most of the time instead of always running up and down the road chasing buckles."

"No kidding! That's wonderful! If…if that's what you want."

"That's exactly what I want," he told her emphatically. "It's the dream, sweetheart, the whole enchilada, everything I love, you, Matthew…" He stroked one hand over her cheek and the other across the baby's head, hurrying on, "having our own place, doing what I'm made to do and earning a good income at it, living the life. It's everything I've ever wanted."

"Oh, I'm so excited!" She bounced a little on the bed. Matthew grunted as if in agreement.

Shifting closer, Chandler quickly said, "I've had my eye on this little ranch east of Stephenville for some time now, and I've made a couple of phone calls. It's a pretty piece of land and in our price range. House isn't all that, but—"

She pressed a finger to his lips, stopping the flow of his words. "If that's what God has in mind for us, I'm sure we can make it work. When can we go see it?"

He kissed that finger. "Soon."

She smiled and stroked his cheek. "Garrett and the aunties will miss us."

Garrett had proven to be an especially attentive uncle, and the aunties… Odelia was like a girl with a favorite new toy and Hypatia didn't even seem to mind the milk stains on her fine silks. Magnolia, however, was the big surprise. Her calmness and sturdy good sense had been a special blessing to these new parents.

Chandler nodded, so full of love and happiness that he thought he might pop like a balloon. "I'll miss them, too."

But this was best. No one could question that their family needed their own home or that God had made a way for them to have it.

"We'll visit often," Bethany said.

"Whenever we can," Chandler agreed, leaning forward to press his lips to hers.

He could barely believe how God had blessed him!

Back in July his life had been coming apart at the seams. Desperate, he'd fallen to his knees. Then God had lifted him up and set him on the right path, showering him with blessings that he could only have imagined a few short months ago. He'd said as much to Kreger just this past weekend when their paths had briefly crossed. To Chandler's surprise, his one-time partner had agreed to sit down and talk with Chandler and his father in the next couple of days.

That was a conversation Chandler intended to bathe in prayer. He was still hurt by his old friend's actions, but he was going to make one more effort to help Kreger get his life right through Christ Jesus. After all, if he didn't try, who would? Besides, Hub would be with him. Together they would make an impassioned plea and leave the rest to God. With his own life bathed in blessings, Chandler figured it was the least he could do. And the very best.

Matthew let out a contented sigh and blinked blearily at his father. As his eyes drifted closed, his sweet little mouth turned up at the corners.

"Look at that!" Bethany whispered. "He's smiling!"

"I know just how he feels," Chandler told her softly. And, oh, he did.

Magnolia tiptoed away from the bedroom door, dabbing tears from her eyes with the sleeve of her bathrobe. She had awakened to the distant sound of the baby wailing. Whenever they heard him cry, all the sisters were eager to offer assistance, so much so that they'd agreed to take turns. Magnolia was a tad miffed to find that Chandler had arrived home and superseded her. She was even more disappointed to hear Chandler and Bethany speak of moving.

None of the sisters had ever believed that Chandler and his little family would stay on at Chatam House permanently. They had to make their own home sooner or later, and God had obviously ordained the moment. She never ceased marveling at the way God worked.

She supposed that she ought not to be so surprised that He had used a baby to bring Chandler and Bethany together. After all, He had used a babe to bring salvation to a lost world. Still, an infant matchmaker!

Had Bethany not been pregnant and desperate, however, Chandler would never have been moved to marry her. Then he would not have found the one true love God had designed especially for him. It was only right that they follow the path God had laid out for their little family.

But, Stephenville! Oh, how she would miss the little scrap and his parents!

A sudden thought brought her to a halt at the door to the suite. So, Chandler and Bethany and little Matthew would be leaving them soon. That must mean that God was preparing Chatam House for someone new!

Who, she wondered, would God send to them next?

She moved quietly out onto the landing and patted the wall with an approving hand as she trundled by. Whomever God sent their way, Chatam House would be ready. Obviously, He had appointed this place not only as a haven for the lost and desperate, but as a garden where love could take root and grow. And love, Magnolia knew, was the sweetest, most beautiful blossom of all.

They were making quite a bouquet for themselves, the Chatam sisters. Not bad for a trio of old spinsters.

She smiled contentedly as she made her way back to her room, silently praising God in His infinite wisdom.

* * * * *

Dear Reader,

Have you ever feared that you were lost only to find yourself right where you needed to be? Life is like that sometimes. None of the landmarks feel familiar, and you can't seem to recall exactly how you got where you are. Then everything begins to make sense and you suddenly realize that you're right where you want to be.

We may not always know where we are going in this life or why, but as Christians we can trust that God is well aware of the paths we trod and has specific destinations in mind for each of us. Moreover, wherever God takes us, that's always the best place for us to be.

May you enjoy the trip as much as the destination!

God bless,

Arlene James

QUESTIONS FOR DISCUSSION

1. Bethany and Chandler both thought they had solid plans for their lives and were settled on a course. Everything seemed to be wrong; then, suddenly each of their worlds turned upside down. Does God really allow, or even cause, such things to happen?

2. Why would God allow the goals and plans of individuals to be disrupted? What or who might this benefit?

3. Ephesians 6:1-4 gives us the formula for healthy parent-child relationships. Yet, though Chandler's father, Hubner, is pastor, a devout man of God. he and Chandler are continually at odds. How does this happen with Christian people?

4. The aunties believe that there are no real coincidences for Christian people, that God always has a purpose and a plan for His children. Do you agree? Why or why not?

5. If God does have plans for each of us, why do we get off track? Why doesn't He *force* us to follow His paths?

6. Is it possible that both Bethany and Chandler were actually living in God's will when He turned their lives upside down? Why or why not? Does the story of Joseph in the Old Testament have anything to say to this subject?

7. The Bible is replete with admonitions against lying and deception. Although Chandler and Bethany took pains not to lie or ask anyone to lie for them, they did plan to deceive others by letting them think that they had

married far earlier then they actually did. Is this acceptable on any level? Why or why not?

8. Assuming that Bethany would be unwilling to enter into a real marriage with him, Chandler proposed a marriage "in name only." Do you believe God honors such marriages? Why or why not?

9. Chandler believed that he was "called" to rodeo competition by God. What does it mean to be "called" to a purpose by God? Is it possible to be "called" to any profession other than church professions? If so, why would God call His children to a particular profession?

10. Chandler came to believe that being a good example was not enough, that he should have *told* his friend Kreger about Jesus. Do you agree or disagree?

TITLES AVAILABLE NEXT MONTH

Available September 28, 2010

HIS HOLIDAY BRIDE
The Granger Family Ranch
Jillian Hart

YUKON COWBOY
Alaskan Bride Rush
Debra Clopton

MISTLETOE PRAYERS
Marta Perry and Betsy St. Amant

THE MARINE'S BABY
Deb Kastner

SEEKING HIS LOVE
Carrie Turansky

FRESH-START FAMILY
Lisa Mondello

LARGER-PRINT BOOKS!

**GET 2 FREE
LARGER-PRINT NOVELS
PLUS 2 FREE
MYSTERY GIFTS**

Larger-print novels are now available...

LILP10R

HARLEQUIN®

A *Romance*

FOR EVERY MOOD™

Spotlight on

— Inspirational —

Wholesome romances
that touch the heart and soul.

See the next page
to enjoy a sneak peek from
the Love Inspired® inspirational series.

*See below for a sneak peek at
our inspirational line, Love Inspired®.
Introducing HIS HOLIDAY BRIDE
by bestselling author Jillian Hart*

Autumn Granger gave her horse rein to slide toward the town's new sheriff.

"Hey, there." The man in a brand-new Stetson, black T-shirt, jeans and riding boots held up a hand in greeting. He stepped away from his four-wheel drive with "Sheriff" in black on the doors and waded through the grasses. "I'm new around here."

"I'm Autumn Granger."

"Nice to meet you, Miss Granger. I'm Ford Sherman, from Chicago." He knuckled back his hat, revealing the most handsome face she'd ever seen. Big blue eyes contrasted with his sun-tanned complexion.

"I'm guessing you haven't seen much open land. Out here, you've got to keep an eye on cows or they're going to tear your vehicle apart."

"What?" He whipped around. Sure enough, mammoth black-and-white creatures had started to gnaw on his four-wheel drive. They clustered like a mob, mouths and tongues and teeth bent on destruction. One cow tried to pry the wiper off the windshield, another chewed on the side mirror. Several leaned through the open window, licking the seats.

"Move along, little dogie." He didn't know the first thing about cattle.

The entire herd swiveled their heads to study him curiously. Not a single hoof shifted. The animals soon returned to chewing, licking, digging through his possessions.

Autumn laughed, a warm and wonderful sound. "Thanks,

I needed that." She then pulled a bag from behind her saddle and waved it at the cows. "Look what I have, guys. Cookies."

Cows swung in her direction, and dozens of liquid brown eyes brightened with cookie hopes. As she circled the car, the cattle bounded after her. The earth shook with the force of their powerful hooves.

"Next time, you're on your own, city boy." She tipped her hat. The cowgirl stayed on his mind, the sweetest thing he had ever seen.

Will Ford be able to stick it out in the country
to find out more about Autumn?
Find out in HIS HOLIDAY BRIDE
by bestselling author Jillian Hart,
available in October 2010
only from Love Inspired®.